Cammie
Takes Flight

LAURA BEST

NIMBUS
PUBLISHING

To the students and staff of the Halifax School For the Blind
1868–1983

Nimbus Publishing Limited
3731 Mackintosh St, Halifax, NS B3K 5A5
(902) 455-4286 nimbus.ca

This novel is a work of fiction. Names, characters, places, and incidents are either the product of the author's imagination or are used fictitiously.

NB1266

Printed and bound in Canada
Cover Design: Sari Naworynski
Interior Design: Heather Bryan

Library and Archives Canada Cataloguing in Publication

Best, Laura, author
Cammie takes flight / Laura Best.

Issued in print and electronic formats.
ISBN 978-1-77108-467-3 (softcover).— ISBN 978-1-77108-476-5 (HTML)

I. Title.
PS8603.E777C34 2017   jC813'.6   C2016-908044-7
                                 C2016-908045-5

Nimbus Publishing acknowledges the financial support for its publishing activities from the Government of Canada, the Canada Council for the Arts, and from the Province of Nova Scotia. We are pleased to work in partnership with the Province of Nova Scotia to develop and promote our creative industries for the benefit of all Nova Scotians.

MIX
Paper from responsible sources
FSC® C013916

Me, strutting my way into the Halifax School for the Blind with my head held high in the air. Like a book with a whole lot of empty pages, I can hardly wait for my new life to begin. Freedom lets you fly like a bird in the sky, and you don't even want to think about landing, not even when your wings get too tired for flapping. The only person back in Tanner who's worth me caring about is my best friend, Evelyn Merry. And while I'm anxious to hear about the steer his pa bought him right before I left, the rest of Tanner can go take a hike. Like it or lump it, Cammie Turple isn't going to spend her days stuck fast to Tanner — no way, no how.

My new life is looking bright and sparkly, smooth and polished as a string of ocean pearls. I'm just itching to tie up the few loose strings left dangling from my old life — tracking down my mother, for starters, and finding out why she never once came to see me when I was growing up. From there on out, there'll be nothing but smooth sailing for me. I'll be sitting back with my feet up, enticing life to sit up and take notice. Cammie Turple will be someone to be reckoned with. I've got big ideas for the future, plans to be made and new memories to build. Not one of them is going to end up with Aunt Millie or Tanner in the picture.

Chapter One

"I didn't want to talk to just any old spirit, so I said, 'Is Granddaddy here?' And right away, the pointer started moving across the board. James got scared when it stopped on *yes*. It was all I could do to keep him from jumping up from the table — the big old fraidy-cat. 'You can't up and leave in the middle of a séance,' I told him. I mean, really!" Nessa grabs her peach off the table and sinks her teeth into it. I roll my eyes.

The girls at our lunch table act like Nessa's the best entertainment to come along since Gene Kelly. If she could dance like him, she'd have my attention fast enough, but until that happens I'm not much interested. My plate is cleaned, my napkin folded. I'm just waiting for the bell to ring so I can be on my way to English class. Bad enough I'm in the same dorm with Nessa, but did I have to get stuck sitting beside her in the dining room for an entire school year, too? Everything she has is bigger, better. The girls back home in Tanner all think *they're* something. Well, I've got news for them. They can't even hold a candle to Nessa Maxwell. She's got them beat all to pieces. All those times I dreamed about going to blind school, I used to imagine we'd all be friends. But just because you have something in common with someone, like bad eyesight, it doesn't mean you'll want to be friends with them.

"Weren't you scared, even a little bit, Nessa? I would have fainted dead away," croons Jennie, rocking back and forth as she speaks. Jennie would do or say just about anything to worm her way into Nessa's good graces — most of the girls would, in fact, all because they're hoping to be invited to Nessa's for a weekend. Talk about being a back-scratcher. Last year these weekends were a fairly regular occurrence. So far this year, Nessa hasn't asked a single one of them home. I say it's all part of Nessa's plan to be popular.

When all the other girls within earshot agree that they'd be scared too, as though what Nessa just said is enough to leave everybody quivering in their skin, I lose it.

"Oh yeah?" I say, before my brain has time to put the brakes on my tongue. "Well, my best friend back home in Tanner has a dead brother who's been visiting him since he was little. And he didn't need some dumb spirit board to point it out to him either. He just wakes up and sees him standing at the foot of his bed, big as life." Heads turn. Mouths drop open. Someone gasps. Mention a ghost and the whole world wants to hear more. I can feel the burn from all those eyes staring in my direction. Then questions start bouncing around the table like hailstones on a tin roof. Suddenly, nobody cares about Nessa's stupid old spirit board.

"Do you have any proof of this?" asks Nessa, clearing her throat. I'm about to speak up and tell her it's just as believable as her spirit-board story when I snap to my senses. I've been here at the school for only a few weeks, and already I can't be trusted with Evelyn's friendship. I promised him I'd never, ever tell. We even sealed it with spit and rubbed it into the palms of our hands. If you're lucky enough to find someone you can trust with your deepest, darkest secrets, I say you'd best be keeping their secrets in return. Friends like that don't happen along any old day of the week.

"Hey, lighten up a little. I was just kidding. My friend didn't see nothing — I was just making a joke." I give an awkward laugh and reach for my milk, downing the last few drops. I've got no plans to be talking about my old life. Next thing I'll be blabbing my own secrets. Think I want anyone knowing that Aunt Millie used to be a bootlegger, or about the get-togethers in her kitchen every Saturday night? I'm usually tight-lipped about such personal matters. What's wrong with me, blurting things out about Evelyn's brother? Some friend I turned out to be. It's all Nessa's fault, getting everyone worked up about that spirit board of hers.

For a few moments nobody says a word, but then Jennie asks again if Nessa was scared, and that does it — Nessa's mouth kicks into high gear, leaving me in the dust.

"Scared? I wasn't scared at first because I didn't believe it was Granddaddy — not for a minute." Relief coils through me. I managed to skin out of that one. Evelyn's secret is safe and sound. Nessa takes another bite out of her peach while everyone waits for her to continue. "No way was some dumb board going to convince me that Granddaddy was talking through it. What a cruel joke that would be, as much as I loved Granddaddy. So I put it to the test. I said to it, 'If this is Granddaddy, tell me what your nickname for me is.' The board spelled it out plain as day and *that's* when I darn near filled my pants. The only one who knew my special name was Granddaddy himself."

Some of the girls gasp, a few giggle. If Nessa says *Granddaddy* just one more time, I think I'll yank all my hair out by the roots.

"So what was it, dear?" says Tammy, leaning across the table at us.

"What was *what*?" Nessa's innocent act is so put on, it's practically oozing out her skin.

"Now, don't act stunned. Your special name — you didn't say what this special name of yours would be." I want to laugh out loud. No beating around the bush when there's a Newfie in the crowd.

Nessa makes some sucking sounds as she polishes off the peach, then she wipes the juice from her chin. She reminds me of old Herb Winters back home, the way he'd give a swipe to his jaw after spitting out tobacco juice. Can't they all see she's just stalling for time?

"It's private, between Granddaddy and me. Like I told you, no one knows." The girls coax Nessa for an answer. They're not about to back down until she spills the beans. Me, I honestly could care less. I'd just like to catch her in a whopper is all; expose her for the bragger she is.

"Okay, but don't laugh," she says, like it wasn't her plan all along to have them begging her for an answer. A chorus of "We won't laugh!" rings out in the dining room like the bell from All Saints Cathedral. I'm expecting us to be told to quiet down a little. Nessa's mouth is rounded up into a full-fledged grin. Maybe she could get a job as a circus clown one day. "It was Peaches, if you must know — he called me Peaches."

Peaches! I want to laugh right in her face. That is such a lie! When the girls giggle and tell her it's a cute nickname, I can't believe my ears. An eye roll wouldn't do her ridiculous story justice; neither would a big whoop-de-do. Can't they tell she made the whole thing up? Peaches — like that wasn't the first thing to pop into her head when she found herself wedged into a tight squeeze. What do you want to bet that if she'd been smacking on an apple or a banana that would have been her so-called nickname instead?

Maybe there's something wrong with me, but you won't find me cozying up to Nessa Maxwell. Who has time for silly spirit boards, anyway? I've got more important things to occupy my time. Looking for my mother in this big old city, for starters.

"I got it! Bring it back with you next week, Nessa. We'll have our own séance right here," squeals Jane like she's just come up with the plan of the century. If she'd been there the day me and Evelyn concocted a plan to blow up Hux Wagoner's moonshine still, she'd have really had something to be excited about.

"Um…I don't know," says Nessa. "If Mum ever found out — I mean, she doesn't know I've used it. Not to mention what Mr. Allen would do if we got caught."

That last excuse sounds mighty puny. From what I've seen so far, Nessa doesn't much care if she gets into trouble with Mr. Allen. She's always being spoken to about one thing or another. If she spent half as much time practicing the piano as she did in Mr. Allen's office, I bet she wouldn't be hitting the wrong notes at morning assembly. Can't tell me that her daddy being a lawyer doesn't speak to the fact that she only ever ends up with a talking-to. Knowing Nessa is dragging her heels on this gives me the perfect opportunity to show her up for the brag-bag that she is. "You do *have* a spirit board? I mean you really have talked to spirits, right?" I say, putting on an innocent act of my own.

A tiny gasp circles round the table like they can't believe my nerve.

"Fine," snaps Nessa, her voice as crisp as the bread Aunt Millie toasts on the top of the wood stove in the morning. "I'll bring it Monday morning. Be ready to be made a believer, Cammie Turple." Believer, my left foot. I'll be surprised if Nessa even brings this stupid spirit board of hers to school.

The bell rings and we jump to our feet. For a split second, Nessa and I are standing face-to-face. I beat it away from her as fast as I can, following the sea of navy blue tunics in front of me. "Slow down, Cammie," comes a warning as I hurry to get in line. Fine for the supervisor to say; she hasn't spent the last half hour listening to Nessa Maxwell spilling out her stories. I slow to a respectable speed, my face hot from being spoken to. Truth is, I know better than to hurry. *Hurry* isn't a word that gets used here at the school. Hurry is for wide-open spaces, Evelyn and me on our way to the river, moving so fast that he has to hold my hand to make sure I don't stumble over a rock in the path.

I finally get myself situated in line, and I want to groan when I look across and see the snow-white hair of my partner. As her hand slips into mine, I wish that stupid rule about holding hands everywhere we go didn't exist. It's only to help out the blind students anyway. I can get myself around okay so long as I know where I'm going.

"I have albinism," Nessa said the very first time we met — as if this albinism of hers was something I would want to know about. She's not the only one at the school with white hair. "*And* I'm a sight-saving student," she added, like she thought I wouldn't know what that meant just because I was new here.

"Everyone at the school who can see is sight-saving," I stated. I don't know why Nessa thinks it makes *her* special

The day I arrived Mr. Allen showed me around the school. I asked him if I'd be learning Braille, something Mae Cushion put in my head last summer. At the time it got me thinking. Maybe my fingers wouldn't be able to make sense of those little dots she talked about. What a relief when he explained that I'd be reading from large-print books, since I could see regular print. He said it's important for those of us who can see not to strain our eyes, and to save what sight we have.

"I've got some jawbreakers in my locker. Do you want one?" asks Nessa, like two seconds ago I hadn't been a cat's jump away from catching her in a lie.

"No, thank you," I snap. I look straight ahead as the line begins to move. Nessa might've gotten off the hook this time, but I'll trip her up sooner or later. The right time will come and Cammie Turple will be waiting.

Chapter Two

I look over at Ed and smile real big. I'm heading off to my new life and I can't imagine anything sweeter. Having my father drive me to the train station is the cherry on top of it all. I've got on a dress from the Simpson's Sears catalogue. Even Aunt Millie said I didn't look bad when I headed out the door. And getting a compliment out of Aunt Millie is like squeezing tomato juice from a turnip. The sun shines in through the windshield of the truck and I sit up nice and close so I won't miss anything important. We drive past the Merrys' red barn. If Evelyn's out in the dooryard I can't make him out, but I give a small wave just in case. We travel along, just enjoying the ride, when right out of the blue Ed stops the truck by a farmer's field. "Jump on back," he says. I climb on up and sit next to the headboard as if this invitation is nothing out of the ordinary. This is going to be one heck of a ride. Me, Cammie Turple, arriving at the Kentville train station in fine fashion. If that doesn't make people take notice, I don't know what will.

—

"Hang on tight," Ed calls out as we take off down the road. Gravel flies from the tires like sparks spitting from a grindstone. The truck swerves and I grab fast, woo-hooing as we go. The trees all run together, blurred into a gigantic ball of green leaves and blue sky. I hold fast to my glasses to make sure they don't go flying off my face.

If Aunt Millie was here she'd be yapping that Ed's brain is the size of a pea for letting me ride on back — but me, I'm just smiling up a dust storm. I close my eyes and enjoy the ride. Wind blowing through my hair, I shake all thoughts of Aunt Millie right out of my head. This day is too special for me to be thinking about her. When I hear someone clear their throat, my eyes snap open.

Aunt Millie! No matter how bad my eyesight is, I'd recognize that bleached hair from any distance. The hows and whys of the situation are running through my brain like a spring grass fire, and it isn't making a lick of sense. We left Aunt Millie back at the house, wrapped up in her housecoat and holding a cup of tea to her lips. I don't say anything at first. I'm still trying to figure out what she's doing on the back of Ed's truck.

"You're on your own from now on, Miss Smartypants."

"You don't have to worry about me," I snap back. "I'm doing just fine and dandy."

"Guess I didn't do enough for you growing up, giving you a roof over your head when no one else would," she says, pushing my satchel at me.

"Where did you get this?" I left it inside the truck with Ed — I know I did. I start rummaging through my belongings, wondering if she hasn't snitched a few things when I wasn't looking — the envelope with my mother's address on it for starters, the one I've been saving for years. I can't lose that if I plan on finding her one day. I let out a sigh of relief. Everything's in its place.

"Well, if it isn't little Blind-Eyed Cammie sitting over there." I make a strange squeak like a blade of grass when Evelyn Merry presses it between his thumbs and blows. Hux Wagner! He's tipping something to his mouth — a bottle of moonshine, if I were to make an educated guess.

"Just having a little refreshment fer the long trip. A feller's gotta stay refreshed," says Hux, his voice filled with same pleasure you get when you're gnawing your way through a licorice whip.

"You can't go on a trip like this without some refreshments," agrees Aunt Millie. Grabbing Hux's bottle from him, she wipes the top in the crook of her arm before gulping down a mouthful.

"Hey! Evelyn and me blew up your still last spring. You don't even make moonshine anymore." Bad enough Aunt Millie's here, but no stinking way is Ed toting the moonshiner to the Kentville train station if I have any say in it. I'll jump off the back of the truck first.

"You didn't blow up nuthin'," says old Hux, taking another swig from the bottle.

This doesn't make any sense. We blew up Hux's still. Evelyn got hurt. He was in the hospital. "Come on, you two! This is my life — my trip. You're not coming with me!"

"Of course we are. You can't get rid of us that easily," squeals Aunt Millie.

I jump to my feet, ready to put a stop to this foolishness — Hux Wagner and Aunt Millie, of all the things. Expecting a sensible word from either one of them would be as useless as chasing a fart in a windstorm.

"I want you to leave," I state in a business-like manner. When Ed hits a pothole in the road, I tumble forward.

"Get off me, Cammie," groans the soft mass I've landed into.

I suck in air so fast my lungs ache. "Evelyn!" I scramble to my feet. Bandages are wrapped around his head like they were the day I visited him in the hospital. Now I know something's fishy.

"You don't need bandages. You're better now. I saw you just yesterday. We said goodbye at our secret camp!"

"Secret camp? Look who's keeping secrets now," says Aunt Millie. Her voice tells me she's got that owly look about her — head tilted to one side, her eyes big and round. I don't need to be up close to her to know that look.

When Evelyn starts shaking all over, I cry for Aunt Millie to help. But she laughs like we're part of some funny play she's watching.

"Stop the truck, Ed!" I slap my hand on the roof of the cab. Ed steps on the gas and the truck speeds on. "Stop the truck! We're going to run off the road! Ed! Ed!" We race down the road on the back of Ed's truck — Evelyn, Aunt Millie, old Hux Wagner, and me. I'm screaming for Ed to stop but no sound comes out. This isn't how my new life is supposed to go!

I sit up in bed, panting and gasping from the same dream that's been waking me up most every night. Tears running down my cheeks, I can hear someone whispering "Cammie, wake up" in my ear. I reach for the pull-chain to snap on the light, but can't find it. I keep swatting the air. "Cammie, are you okay?"

Slowly I come to my senses. Three weeks and you'd think I'd remember not to reach for the light, that I'm not back home in my old bedroom. Jennie's warm hand traces the stream of tears to my chin.

"I'm fine," I say, pushing her hand away. I quickly wipe the water from my face. I can't figure out how she finds me in the dark. I guess when you're totally blind, nighttime doesn't stop you from getting around. If I were in her shoes, not able to see a thing, I'd never leave my bed — guaranteed.

I roll onto my side and try to go back to sleep. My chest makes two quick heaves and I snuff the snot back up my nose in the way that annoys the pants off Aunt Millie. Tears are building behind my eyes again, but I'm not about to let the dam burst open. Finally I sit up in bed, and I picture my bedroom back home in Tanner; the way the full moon comes up over the trees and shines across my bed. I think about the night Evelyn climbed in through my bedroom window. But then right away I remember it was the same night his pa got drunk and chased him out of the house with the shotgun. A gulp of air gets caught in my throat and I don't know how to get it out. I can't stop thinking about Evelyn, all those days he spent in the hospital out cold. He wouldn't have blown up Hux's moonshine still if it hadn't been for me. Now I'm in the city living a new life while he's stuck back in Tanner. I give a big sigh. What I wouldn't give to spend a day at our secret camp by the river, just Evelyn and me.

Flopping back onto the bed, I stare up at the ceiling and try to put my mind on other things. Reaching under my mattress, I pull the envelope out and hold it close. If it wasn't for the letter she wrote Aunt Millie years ago, I wouldn't have a clue about where to start my search for mother dearest. Too bad Aunt Millie burned the letter when I was a kid, like she didn't think I'd be interested in hearing what my mother had to say. At least I have the envelope — not much, but something. *Burnham Street, Halifax, Nova Scotia*, big as you please, written on the envelope I've been carrying around with me since forever, still with no plans of how I'm going to get there. It's not like I can just up and walk there. Heck, I wouldn't even make it out the front door without getting caught. I've got time on my side, though. A whole school year if need be. And with nearly twelve years of biding my time, I'll wait as long as I have to. Sooner or later, opportunity will come knocking at my door.

Putting the envelope back in its hiding place, I turn toward the wall and swallow the hard lump in my throat. I never in a million years thought I'd miss anything about my old life back in Tanner. You can dress your life up all you want, forget about who you used to be, but getting rid of the past isn't as easy as taking off your dirty old underwear and kicking it under the bed.

Chapter Three

"Telephone call for Vanessa Maxwell."

Not again! I blow a ball of air out of my mouth. Figures she'd be the one getting all the telephone calls. Must be nice to be *that* important. Someone called for her just the other day, too. As Nessa breezes out past the bunks, the girls in the dorm coo and go on something wicked.

"What do you want to bet it's Frankie Parker on the other end of that line?" says Jane, giggling that high-pitched laugh of hers. Frankie Parker — now that's a ridiculous statement if I ever heard one. The school keeps the boys and girls as far apart as they can. If they could use a ten-foot pole for a marker they probably would. The boys sit on the other side of the classroom, and when we change classes they've got their own side of the hallway, too. Dining room — it's the same deal. Dormitory — forget it, they're on the other side of the building. They even have their own playground. Get caught hanging out near the fence and you're likely to get booted out of there in a hurry. And if all that isn't enough, there's only one pay station in the entire school. There's no way Frankie Parker, or any other boy for that matter, could call. Impossible.

"You can't be serious," I say to Jane. If you're making a statement you'd best be prepared to back it up with proof.

The dorm rings with laughter like it's a big joke on me. The girls back in Tanner used to laugh whenever I was within earshot — mean laughs that told me I'd never belong in their group. *Not here too*, I want to cry, *the only place in the world I ever thought I'd fit in.* For a moment my face stings like a cut rolled in iodine, but then Jennie motions for me to come close. My heart expands and sighs with relief. It wasn't a mean-spirited laugh after all.

I scooch on over to Jennie's bed while the other girls close in on us. She smells like the lavender powder her grandmother sent her last week. I look over the top of her brown head — naturally curly. The maids complain about how hard it is to comb, but I'd do anything to have hair like that. Resisting the urge to touch it, I snap back to attention. Jennie's about to let me in on a well-kept secret. I don't need any distractions. She tells me to cross my heart and hope to die and stick a needle in my eye. I'm not going to go sticking a needle in my eye or hoping to die at my age, but I go along with the promise because I'm anxious to get the real scoop.

"Is the coast clear?" asks Jennie before continuing.

Tammy looks toward the doorway and gives the all-clear.

"The boys sneak out and use the pay phone down at the corner. But you can't tell a living soul. Not now. Not ever."

Right away my logical mind is saying that's next to impossible. A mouse couldn't sneak out of here. I'm sure of it. I look around at the faces in front of me. Tammy's nodding and smiling like a pumpkin grinner. For a few moments I'm not sure what to think. That's when it finally hits me.

"Yeah, right. Sneak out of the school! You just about had me there." I fall back on the bed laughing like a loon.

"Jennie's telling the truth," pipes in Amy. Amy doesn't strike me as the type to make up stories.

"At least we get to talk with the boys that way," says Tammy.

"Joe Banks used to call *me* last year," says Amy, like maybe that makes her the envy of everyone here. Me, I could envy her for her height alone — the tallest girl in our dorm even in her stocking feet.

"Hey, he called me, too!" says Vicki with a giggle.

"He's got a whiny voice," says Amy, pinching her nose while she talks, "and keeps saying, 'Isn't it so…isn't it so.'" It's Amy's turn to laugh this time.

While the girls jabber on about the boys, I'm making a quick calculation of this juicy bit of information. This is the very thing I've been hoping for. So, there *is* a way out of here! I want to throw my arms into the air and shout for joy. I'll find my mother yet. Knowing there's a way for me to get the very thing I want spreads a grin out across my face. Things are looking up for Cammie Turple.

Sometimes you need to keep your plans in the hatching stage for a time. You've got to let them ripen to the point where they're ready to pop on their own. Determination has mighty long legs. It brought me all the way to Halifax. A few more steps and it might just take me to Burnham Street, and land me right on my mother's doorstep. Too bad there's only a street name on the envelope. But I'll knock on doors if I have to. Someone living on that street must know her. One way or another I'll track her down and have it out with her, find out why she dumped me out with a bootlegger and walked away. Finally, I'll get the answers to all my questions.

A year ago I wouldn't have imagined any of this was possible. I was just a kid bellyaching about hard times and hoping things would work out all on their own. Nothing ever works out without you doing something about it. Now, that's something I learned from Evelyn Merry. After we took matters into our own hands, I found out Ed was my real father, Aunt Millie stopped selling moonshine, and Evelyn's pa even got himself straightened out. Who knew that under all the moonshine was a respectable man all clean-shaven and dapper? Too bad his other son getting drowned turned him into a miserable human being all those years before. Aunt Millie said being faced with losing another son brought Jim Merry back to his own good senses. Every once in a while Aunt Millie knows what she's talking about.

This whole business about the boys sneaking their way out of the school plays on my mind the rest of the evening. While it means escape is possible, I'm not sure I could slip out all on my own without getting caught. Not to mention that I don't have a clue as to where Burnham Street is or how to get there. Tanner might be small, but at least I can make my way around even with my bad eyes. Halifax is a whole other story. How can I find anything in this big old city with only me, myself, and I to figure it out? Everything's so new. I'm just getting used to the inside of the school, figuring out what everything is and how to get where I want to go. The buildings here are tall and the streets all look the same. I'd be lost in no time. While I'm anxious to find my mother, I've got to slow down and think this through.

I start to wonder if one of the boys would be willing to help me out. Seeing as how I don't know a single one of them, I'm not at all sure. Last week a ball of paper skidded across my desk in Mrs. Christi's classroom. Careful not to make any noise, I straightened out the wrinkles and held it up to read — all that without missing a spelling word. I quickly found out the note was for Vicki and it was from Henry Fields, which was probably a good thing since he's all Vicki talks about. No wonder she'd get a note. While I'm not one for commenting on people's looks, I've heard what the other girls have to say — that Vicki could pass for Vivien Leigh's daughter. Not just anyone gets compared to a Hollywood starlet.

With Mrs. Christi being as blind as a newborn kitten, maybe a note will work for me. But what would I write? "I need to get out of here and find my mother who lives on Burnham Street" sounds dumb and "Can you get me out of here?" sounds like a note of desperation. With a bit of thought I can come up with just the right words. I know I can. But will the boys even let me in on this escape route of theirs? Could be it's top secret. And they might not want to help out a stranger for free.

For now, I'll have to let this idea of sneaking out of the school simmer a little longer. Back home, Evelyn and me would put our heads together and come up with a plan. But I'm a Turple and that means I've got plenty of ingenuity, and sooner or later I'll think of something. I've waited for nearly twelve years to find my mother. What's a few more days going to hurt?

Chapter Four

"I'll stand guard," I say, zipping toward the doorway. Nessa's just made the grand announcement that it's time to get out the spirit board.

"You're going to miss out on the fun," giggles Jennie, rocking back and forth on the bed. "Aren't you the least bit curious? I mean, talking to ghosts. I've got goose bumps just thinking about it." Her laughter is as twisted as a peppermint stick, like she's thrilled and scared all at the same time. I don't know why she's so all-fired excited about this séance business. It's not like she'll be able to see what's going on. But I can't point that out to her. No one wants you stating their shortcomings.

One thing I'll say, Jennie can sure make you forget that she's blind. She's no slouch when it comes to manual training class. She can knit slicker than those of us who can see. And she's not all the time asking for help, neither. I don't think she ever drops a stitch. Me, I've dropped more stitches than I've knitted. I try picking them up without Mrs. Willow's help, but dropped stitches are hard to see. If things don't improve, I'm going to see about trying something else. Knitting's not the only thing they've got here. I could take up crocheting, maybe even learn to make baskets. There's got to be something I'm good at.

"I see what I need to do in my head and then I just go do it," Jennie said, showing me the doll she'd just knitted. I told her that took both brains *and* talent, and there's probably hope for all of us here.

"You go ahead. Someone has to keep watch," I say, ignoring the look of disappointment on Jennie's face. Talking to the dead sounds like it might be fun, but what does Nessa really know about the spirit world? Evelyn, he'd be right up for it. No questions asked. But then, he's been seeing his dead brother since he was small. I'm not nearly as brave as Evelyn.

Miss Turner made her rounds a few minutes ago. It'll be some time before I hear the clicking of her shoes in the hallway. She's probably in the supervisor's lounge right about now. She shouldn't be back until lights out if everything goes as planned. But this whole séance business could end up being a flop. Not that I won't feel happy if Nessa gets herself caught up in a big snag and carted off to Mr. Allen's office to do some explaining.

The girls are chattering like chipmunks. Me, I'm in position by the doorway staring out at the bare walls. And then, one voice rises to the surface like a burp after a great big meal. Before you know it, Nessa's telling everyone what to do and where to stand. Leaning against the door with a good view of the hallway, I'm glad not to be bossed around by Nessa. Arms crossed in front of me, I take the opportunity to peek over my shoulder. Nessa marches over to her wardrobe and opens the door.

She sure didn't waste any time proving me wrong. As promised, she snuck the spirit board to school on Monday morning when her father dropped her off for the week. She agreed to have a séance on Friday, but the girls kept begging her to take it out before then.

"I said Friday and I meant Friday," Nessa said, like she enjoyed having something to dangle in front of everyone.

All week long the dorm has been like a beehive, with everyone buzzing about what all they'll ask the board when or if Nessa gives them a chance. Most questions concern the boys: who likes who, and all that silly stuff I don't go in for. Some of them plan on asking dumb things like the name of their dog or what their favourite colour is. I say if you're going to be pestering ghosts, you'd best have something of the utmost importance on your mind. So for that reason I've got no interest — not to mention the board belongs to Nessa. Besides, who's to say the whole thing isn't a bunch of malarkey? A board that can answer every question you could think of asking, even see into your future before it's happened — I have to wonder if that's possible. I mean, if it is, you might just as well sit back and let life happen. No sense in coming up with any plans of your own.

"Time to see how many spirits are out there," Nessa says like the expert she's convinced everyone she is. She tells me to turn out the lights so we can create the right atmosphere. "Ghosts don't like it too bright. That's why they only come out at night."

I'm not sure what all ghosts like and what they don't, but I turn off the lights because not only am I keeping guard but I'm also a whisker away from the switch. I've got no excuse. A series of protests ring out as soon as everything becomes dim.

"I can't see the letters on the board."

"Get in closer."

"There's not enough light."

"Wait till your eyes adjust. And quiet down or you'll scare the ghosts away. They don't like loud noises, either."

Everyone hushes. The expert has spoken.

"I still can't see," someone whispers.

"Fine, then. We'll leave the lights on," Nessa snaps. I

laugh to myself as I hit the switch again. Nessa thinking she can pull off a séance here at the school — as if.

"It's time to warm up the board," states Nessa. "We'll ask some easy questions to begin with, ones we know the answer to. As a test."

Nessa and Tammy are the first to have a go. "Oohs" and "aahs" vibrate in the air as soon as they start shooting the question at the spirit board. Good grief. Like none of us knew today was Friday and that we ate fish for supper. Fish is always served on Friday. Even a dead person should know that much. Wouldn't you think someone could come up with some important questions? I'd be asking things like: *What's the meaning of life?* and *Do babies that die before they're baptized get a free pass into heaven?* Instead of that all-important question, *Will Frankie Parker sneak a kiss from Nessa at the Christmas dance?* I can't believe Tammy just asked that. Before Nessa has time to find out the answer, there comes a loud thump inside the dorm. Confusion erupts like a volcano, and in no time flat a racket breaks out. I can't make sense of what's going on until Tammy cries out that Jennie's having another one of her fits. A gaggle of girls come running toward me, squealing and yelling like banshees.

"Jennie's down!"

"Get the supervisor!"

"Get a spoon! She'll swallow her tongue!"

I take off in a flash, running down the hallway, calling out for help. Quicker than a finger-snap, Miss Turner is on the scene.

"Jennie's having another fit. She fell on the floor this time." My words run together like a string of farts. I'm surprised that Miss Turner can decipher what I've just said.

"Seizure, Cammie — we call them seizures."

Seizures or fits or whatever you want to call them; in the few weeks since I've been at the school Jennie has had two of them, but she didn't land on the floor those times. They don't last for long, a few minutes tops, but it's scary all the same.

Before you can say, "spirit board," Miss Turner is in the dorm and taking control of the situation. She tells everyone to step back. Nessa's spirit board has mysteriously disappeared and she's making out she doesn't know what Jennie was doing right before she took her fit.

"Seizure," corrects Miss Turner. She inspects Jennie from head to toe to make sure she doesn't have any bumps or bruises even though Jennie insists that she's fine, just fine. "I've got the worst headache, though," she adds.

Taking Jennie's hand, Miss Turner slowly helps her up off the floor. As soon as Miss Turner goes off to the infirmary to get some Aspirin, Jennie starts apologizing for ruining the séance.

"Too bad it had to happen before it answered the last question," giggles Nessa.

"It's not like she can help it," I state. I can't believe the gall. Who cares about Nessa getting kissed, anyway?

"We know she can't help it," says Tammy. "Nessa just meant —"

"Some things are more important than boys and stupid spirit boards," I cut in.

"It's okay, Cammie," says Jennie, kind of mousey-like. "Really it is. I know what they mean." She sounds as though she could start crying at any moment.

Having the kibosh put to Nessa's séance doesn't make me feel the least bit sorry, even though I can't say much for the way it came about. Poor Jennie. Being totally blind is one thing. Taking fits on top of all that is adding insult to injury. What have I got to complain about? Nessa Maxwell and her bossy tendencies, that's all. A knot starts growing in my throat as I look at Jennie. I hurry away to find a little privacy, a little time just for me.

Life sure has a funny way of giving you what you want.

Chapter Five

Just as I'm about to tell Evelyn Merry about Nessa's stupid séance flop, Miss Turner interrupts my thoughts. It takes a few seconds for what she's saying to sink in.

"Yes, Cammie — there's a telephone call for you." The words sound like honey dripping off her lips. My heart hiccoughs. I scoop up the letter I'm writing, faster than Evelyn Merry can crack a whip, and put it in my locker. Clamping my lips tight, I head down to the pay station. There's a smile beaming inside me that I don't want to show. I can't make myself out to be an amateur in front of everyone, like I've never in the world ever talked on the telephone before.

My mind starts guessing who could be calling. It can't be one of the boys — that's for sure. Besides, Nessa seems to have that market cornered. Last week she got a total of three telephone calls. Each time she came back to the dorm claiming the call was from a different boy. Like anyone would believe that. I haven't been close enough to any of the boys to even say hello, let alone get a telephone call from one of them. I'm still working up the courage to ask one of them to help me sneak out of here. Taking all this into consideration, I can't decide if getting a telephone call is a good thing or a bad thing. Bad news comes by telegraph. That old busybody Mae Cushion still goes on about all the telegraphs that were sent out when the war was on. Seeing as how one of them got delivered to her own house, I suppose that's to be expected. Finding out your son isn't going to come home can't be easy. Maybe bad news comes over the telephone lines, too. But that's just silly. Who would be calling me at all, let alone someone with bad news? I tell my head to smarten up as I make my way along.

While the telephone lines were run though Tanner way before I was born, Aunt Millie could never be bothered to get connected. "What do I need a telephone for?" she'd sometimes say. The few times she used one, she'd gone up the road to old Genie Radcliff's and, because she wasn't sure Genie would let her use her telephone, she'd drag me along.

"Pucker up and make yourself look pitiful. You're good at that," she'd say before knocking on Genie's door. "Genie's a sucker for a sob story. We'll just tell her you're not feeling good and I'm putting in a call to the doctor."

"Aunt Millie," I'd whine, wondering how I was supposed to make myself look sickly at the snap of a finger.

"Oh, hush now, Cammie. I've seen you put on that pitiful look when it suited you."

We'd go into a little room where Genie's telephone was mounted on the wall. Once we were in complete privacy, Aunt Millie would ring Central and give them the number she wanted to call.

"Keep your ears plugged," she'd sometimes say to me. When she was through, she'd ring the operator back up and ask what the charges were, dig into her dress pocket for the change, and hand it over to Genie before we left. She'd gush on about how generous it was of Genie to allow her to use the telephone, and how sickly I was.

"She does look pale," Genie would agree.

I bet Genie wouldn't have been so free-hearted about letting Aunt Millie use her telephone if she knew those calls were really going out to some Ray or Ted or Harvey over in Sheppard Square. Aunt Millie was never bashful about telling lies. I guess when you're a born liar, it's an everyday occurrence in your life just like breathing or digesting your food.

The queasy feeling in the pit of my stomach is hard to ignore. I pick up the receiver and hold it to my ear. I say hello, the way Aunt Millie did, only I don't make my voice sound all syrupy the way she used to. There's loud crackling on the other end like a cat scratching on a fence post.

"Hello," I repeat, wondering at this point if someone isn't playing a prank on me. I don't know a thing about using one of these contraptions. I can't help feeling dumb. Forget the fact that it's awkward standing at the pay station with a telephone receiver stuck up to my ear — anyone passing by will hear what I have to say. Just as I'm considering hanging up, words start reaching my ears. The voice on the other end sounds a million miles away. It's mixed in between the snaps, crackles, and scratches already dancing on the line.

"Cam…is…you? It's aun…mill…"

"Who *is* this?" I ask, wishing whoever it is they'd speak up. Seconds later the crackling stops.

"Who in Sam Hill do you think it is? I was just about to hang up. Me, running up long-distance changes on dead air. What do you think I am, a millionaire?" The words leap into the telephone receiver, sending the little bird in my chest somersaulting inside of me.

"Aunt Millie?" Blood rushes to my ears, making small thumps against my eardrums. My brain is going a billion miles an hour. The fact that Aunt Millie is telephoning me at all is enough to kick-start my heart.

"Well, it's not the Queen of England."

"Has something happened? Is Evelyn okay?"

"Don't worry about that Merry boy. He's making out okay. Besides, I didn't call about that." Relief blusters through me like the hurricane that destroyed Jim Merry's chicken coop last year. But then, right away I'm annoyed at Aunt Millie for elbowing her way into my new life. It's not like she wanted me to come here to school. She did everything she could to stop me, convincing Ed I was better off not knowing he was my father. And all because she knew he'd give permission for me to come.

"What do you want, then?" I ask with a mouth full of sassiness.

"I'm not so bad, now that you've asked. 'I dare say I've missed you, Aunt Millie. How are you? Is life treating you kindly?'" That snotty tone in her voice is impossible to miss. If I ever said any of those polite things to her she'd ask me if I was running a fever.

"So...How *are* you?" I drag the question out like a wrung-out dishrag. "Well, excuse me for thinking that you might actually be glad to hear your dear sweet aunt's voice after all these weeks." Dear sweet aunt? What a laugh. She sounds as though she's hurt, but then quickly changes gears. "Aren't you wondering where I'm calling from? Drew just got the telephone hooked up a week ago." She sounds pleased. I can hear a smile building in her voice.

Drew Bordmann. I let out a grunt. I was hoping he'd be out of her life by now. But seeing how I'm in the big city, I'm the last person who should have a say in what goes on back in Tanner. "Full steam ahead," as Herb Winters used to say. And I'm not looking anywhere but forward.

"I told you I'd be getting a telephone hooked up before you took off for Halifax. I'm sure you don't remember any of that, though. You never do pay attention to what I've got to say."

Her getting a telephone doesn't affect me any more than her giving up bootlegging. I've been busy living my own life, not wondering what she's been up to these days. If I could keep her out of my dreams at night I'd be all set.

There's dead air for a time. "Why did you say you were calling?" I finally ask. It isn't like Aunt Millie to beat around the bush. She usually blurts things out and worries about what she's said later.

"I was wondering if you've heard from Ed."

"Ed? Has something happened to Ed?" My heart beats out a fine tune on my ribs. Not Ed, not when I just learned he was my father a few months back.

"No, nothing's wrong with Ed that a swift kick wouldn't fix."

"That's not very nice," I say coldly. Leave it to Aunt Millie to say something mean about a person the moment she's a teensy bit annoyed.

"Ed's making trouble for us. I think I've got a right to be 'not very nice.'"

"Trouble? For us?" I've been around enough troublemakers in my life to know that Ed isn't one of them.

"That's what I said." Her voice is prickly like the bark on a hawthorn bush. Talk about touchy.

"What kind of trouble?" Whatever she has to say will be ridiculous. I can bet on it. Aunt Millie can stretch the truth out like molasses candy. Too bad her truth always ends up tasting bitter.

"He's butting into things that are none of his concern. It's not like he was around when you were growing up. No — he was off gallivanting around the countryside having a time for himself, free as a bird, not a care in the world."

My voice grows loud with anger as I say, "He was fighting in the war, in case you forgot," which I know she hasn't. I look around to see if anyone is handy enough to have heard me. She's got no business criticizing Ed. Her own sister is a shining example of how to be a lousy parent. "Besides, it's not like mother dearest told him about me," I add, lowering my voice.

"Now, don't get fresh with me, young lady. Just because Ed Hanover decides he wants to be involved in your life it doesn't give him the right to go poking around the past. There's no point in dredging all that old stuff up anyway."

I sigh. "What does this have to do with me now?"

"Maybe nothing. Maybe a lot. You never know what'll happen when people start snooping in your business. I thought maybe he came to see you, asked what you thought about adoption."

"Adoption? Ed wants to adopt a baby?" This whole telephone conversation is making less and less sense all the time.

"Not a baby. You, knucklehead. He wants to adopt you."

A big swallow catches up in my throat as I croak out, "Ed wants to adopt me?" People adopt babies, not kids who are going on twelve. Besides, he's my real father. Why would he have to adopt me?

"That's what I just said — you. Oh, he's got these big plans. Wants to change your last name to Hanover. Move you out to Sheppard Square with him and Miranda."

"Miranda?" I don't know why, but hearing that feels strange. I've never thought about Ed having someone in his life.

"That's what I said — Miranda. Says he's getting married and settling down. Says he thinks he can make things up to you, like any of that's ever going to work out for him." There's that mocking tone in her voice again. I hate the babyish way she says Miranda's name, like she's jealous that Ed's finally found someone.

"What did you tell him?"

"I flat-out told him he can't have you. 'Cammie's mine,' is what I said. 'Who changed her dirty diapers and spent nights walking the floor?' I told him. I brought you up through all the hard years, taught you right from wrong, and he thinks now he can just step in and take over from here. Well, he's got another think coming, he has."

"Right from wrong?" I can hardly believe my ears. My eyes are rolling in my head like marbles in the schoolyard. Living with Aunt Millie, I've seen and heard enough wrong to last a lifetime.

"You never got into trouble like the other kids around Tanner, did you? Why? Because you knew there'd be consequences waiting for you if you did. I promised Brenda from the beginning that I'd make you toe the line."

"Look, I've got to go. It's bath night and I can't be late." If my patience gets any thinner I'll pop like an overblown balloon right here on the spot.

"Listen up, now: if Ed *does* come around, this is what I want you to tell —"

I hang up the telephone with Aunt Millie still clacking away on the other end. "Can't have me!" I grunt. Like she owns me. Like me living with her for the first almost twelve years of my life gives her some special hold on me. Aunt Millie's never happy unless she's scrapping with someone. This week it's Ed. Next week it could be the Watkins man from over in Sheppard Square, although I doubt that since he's been giving her free product samples for years.

I stomp away from the pay station. Even when I'm away from her, Aunt Millie tries to mess things up one way or another. I should have known as much. Bad enough she keeps interrupting my sleep at night. Why call me up and start in on Ed? Well, she and Ed will have to settle things among themselves. Besides, she should be happy to have Ed take me off her hands. She threatened to send me to the orphan house plenty of times over the years. Guess all those times she was just blowing hot air.

Aunt Millie doesn't want the past dredged up; big wonder. She'd have to admit her own sister is a miserable excuse for a mother. Even Aunt Millie, with all her faults, has been a better mother to me than Brenda could ever dream of being. And that's not saying a whole lot. A dead tree stump could have done a better job than Brenda.

Knowing my mother's living in the city someplace makes me a little antsy. We could pass each other on the street and I'd never know. Hope gets stirred up in you when you're small. All those years of thinking she'd one day come for me are a thing of the past. I'm doing just great without her. She had no right to leave me behind. One way or another I'll track her down and tell her so. It's a matter of principle. I'm not looking for some loving reunion with her, expecting her to be a mother. Sometimes you just want to see things for yourself, get to know the truth on your own terms.

The spite in me continues to build into something powerful and ugly as I hurry toward the washroom. Just let me get caught for running right about now — see if I give a care.

Chapter Six

Leaning in toward the mirror, I stick out my tongue and make the ugliest face imaginable while preparing to let myself have it with a blast of plain old reality. I'm spiteful and need to get a few things off my chest. It's something I should have done when I was little instead of hanging on to the hope that Aunt Millie spun for me over the years — pretending that my mother was going to come home one day to get me. As if!

If I could go back in time and see myself whining to Aunt Millie, asking her when my mother was going to show up, I'd set myself straight. I'm fed up feeling sorry for myself. And I've got news for my younger self.

Words fly out of me like goose dung as spite spins off the tip of my tongue.

"Grow up, kid. Get over it. Your mother's not here — so what? She's making her mark, living it up, having a grand old time. Think she'll come back for you someday? Well, fat chance of that ever happening. Consider yourself lucky some bootlegger gave you a home. That's all you deserve. Who'd want you, anyway? Get tough and get over it."

To end things off, I spit at the mirror and thumb my nose. "Take that, you big old baby!" I lean against the sink, drained and limp as a wilted flower — but in a peaceful sort of way. Never did I imagine that speaking the truth like that could give you such a load of satisfaction.

A split second later, laughter bounces off the ceiling behind me. I let out a gasp, covering my mouth with my hands. My skin settles to the floor right after I jump out of it. Someone has been stealing a listen at my deepest, darkest secrets. Face hot and burning, shame shakes a cold finger at me. My secret is out — my innermost thoughts. Everyone will know. Just like back in Tanner, I'll be the laughingstock of the whole school: *Poor little Cammie Turple, the bootlegger's niece!*

"Who were you talking to, Cammie?"

I'd recognize that voice any day. I whirl around, trying to take up as much space as I can whilst preparing to face my enemy. Figures that of all the people who could hear my deepest, darkest secrets, it would end up being Nessa "Big Mouth" Maxwell.

"What are you doing in here?" I bark. "Can't a person get an ounce of privacy?" Nastiness spins inside me like a top. I've never used my fists before, but there's a first time for everything.

"I heard someone shouting. So I came to see what was going on."

Nessa's not fooling me, covering up her nosiness by sounding concerned. I swallow at the lump in my throat, but it won't budge.

"You eavesdropping for some particular reason?" I ask, trying to sound as tough as one of Aunt Millie's pie crusts. It's a trick I picked up from watching Aunt Millie through the years. It always worked when there was someone standing outside the backdoor late at night, three sheets to the wind. I hope by now Nessa is shivering in her shoes.

"I thought someone might need help — that's all. *Excuse me* for being concerned." I detect a nip of pleasure in her voice. If she's frightened by what I just said, she's doing a fine job of hiding it. I can just imagine the fun she'll have blabbing all this to everyone. *Poor Cammie doesn't know where her mother is.* The other girls will think it's the funniest thing they've ever heard.

"Well, next time just mind your own beeswax."

I knock into her on purpose as I hurry out past. I don't wait to hear what she has to say about that. When I get back to the dormitory, a few girls are crammed around Jennie's bed like birds to bread crumbs, cooing over the verses in her autograph album. You'd think she just got herself a signed autograph from Lefty Frizzell or some big Hollywood starlet.

"Do you want to see it, Cammie?" asks Amy. "Tammy just wrote the funniest verse in Jennie's album."

"Sorry, I'll miss my bath," I say, heading toward my wardrobe. Not that a bath is that important to me, but at least it'll give me something to think about other than Aunt Millie's telephone call. Not to mention Nessa hearing my entire life story.

Nessa is standing beside my wardrobe. I don't much like having her for a shadow, so I reach in and grab my bathrobe without saying a word. The telephone call from Aunt Millie rolls around in my head as I carry on with my business. I can't imagine why Ed would suddenly be talking about adopting me. This coming from Aunt Millie, can it even be believed? Aunt Millie's words have a way of digging their nails in deep. Maybe this is her way of making *my* life miserable. It's not like she was happy for me to be coming here to school. Heck, she put up a fuss about me going to regular school back in Tanner. At home I'd push things away, keep them for later when I was alone in bed at night. Here at the school you're almost never alone.

The water faucet makes a squeak. The tub fills up slowly. I kneel on the floor and stick my hand under the running water. I spent my whole life wondering why my parents never came to see me, and now that I've finally discovered who my father is, Aunt Millie's trying to take that away from me too. Ed wants to be a part of my life. Is that so hard for her to believe?

My big toe reaches out to test the water. Perfect. Lowering myself in, I soap up the facecloth, cleaning my face, ears, and neck as I go.

"I'll scrub your back," the maid says. Her joints creek as she squats on the floor beside the tub. Handing her the washcloth, I draw my legs up and round my back for good scrubbing. Hunched over, face pushed into my knees, my chest makes a funny heave — another and another. Tears roll down my cheeks before I can stop them from slithering out. I don't even know if this news about Ed makes me happy or sad.

"Are you crying?" the maid asks.

I nod. I know it's no good to lie.

Chapter Seven

Last evening I wrote a note in big black letters and slipped it into my spelling notebook. "Who can take me to Burnham Street?"

That telephone call from Aunt Millie just made me more determined to track down Brenda and rub her nose in the fact that Ed wants to adopt me, that I've got one parent in my life who cares about me even if she doesn't.

I wait for my own good sense to tell when the time is right to put my plan in gear. Mrs. Christi calls out our spelling words and I breeze through some of the easy ones. Slipping the note out, I can't deny that I'm a bit anxious as I scrunch up the paper for good tossing. I wait for just the right moment, for Mrs. Christi's ugly brown dress to swoosh past. The next word she gives us to print out is the word *ridiculous*. I take careful aim, count a quick one, two, three in my head, and send the note across the room.

Seconds after takeoff, Mrs. Christi takes a step backward. I hold my breath. I see movement on the other side of the room. The note must have missed her. A skirmish takes place; the quick squeak of shoes against the floor. I wish I could see what's going on. I can only imagine the boys are clamouring to get their hands on my note. This isn't the first message to make its way to their side of the classroom. While it would seem the next step is to wait for a reply, I get a big surprise when I pick up my pencil and start printing.

"Barry," says Mrs. Christi, her voice cutting through the classroom like a hand scythe through harvest wheat. "Would you please read the note that just sailed past my head?"

My heart pushes into my cheeks and ears. Mrs. Christi's shoes make hollow sounds on the floor as she paces slowly back and forth. I'm busted! I'll be tossed out on my ear, sent off to Mr. Allen's office and from there back to Aunt Millie.

I can't help feeling antsy at the sound of the paper being smoothed out. Barry Huphman clears his throat before reading my note out loud. A short silence follows.

"Burnham Street? How interesting," says Mrs. Christi. "And who penned this note?" Laughter rings out. "Quiet, children," comes a quick warning. I'm a finger's width away from being found out, from having my name read out in front of everyone. Heat climbs down my neck as I imagine Mr. Allen's accusations tumbling down on me.

"It's not signed," says Barry, sounding as surprised as I'm feeling at the moment. I can make out the sound of him turning the note over, the crinkling of paper.

Not signed! Impossible. I checked that note over three times last night. I signed my full name. I know I did. Then like a flash of lightning it hits me: Barry lied to save my skin. That has to be one of the nicest things anyone has ever done for me. I'm so relieved my toes are tingling. I want to rush to the boys' side and kiss Barry Huphman right in front of everyone. Sometimes having your well-thought-out plan backfire on you ends up being a stroke of good luck. One thing's for sure: for a blind person, Mrs. Christi can sure see a lot.

The cafeteria buzzes at lunchtime. Everyone wants to know who wrote the note. Me, my lips are sealed. I look over and see Nessa giving me the eyeball, like she's considering it might have been me, and I get an odd feeling inside. But then she starts yapping about the picture show she saw last Saturday evening and I relax. As for my plan, I'll have to come up with another line of attack. Brenda's not getting off the hook that easily.

"I keep telling her I can't eat candy all day long, but she keeps packing it in my bag all the same," Nessa says all breezy — like it's no big deal. I'm not sure if she's calling attention to the fact that she can get her hands on all the candy in the world or that she gets to go home on weekends. Seems to me there are plenty of worthwhile things to complain about in life — having too much candy isn't one of them. Nessa pulls out a brown paper bag and tosses some candy on top of her bed. The girls look like chickens out in the dooryard the way they're scrambling after the sweets — five or six of them going at it all at once. I guess they don't care how ridiculous they look.

Not that I'm one for pointing out other people's faults, but I can't help noticing that Nessa likes being in control. She reminds me too much of Aunt Millie in that respect for me to be sociable with her. Not to mention I've been waiting for her to shoot her mouth off and tell everyone what she heard the other day in the washroom. Nearly a week after the fact and she hasn't peeped a word about it. I'd like to say I'm impressed, but I know she's just biding her time. Things like that usually have sizeable teeth that come back to bite you in the rear end. No doubt she's waiting for just the right moment to blab it around that Cammie Turple has a habit of talking to herself. Talking to yourself means you either have money in the bank or else you're crazy. I'm pretty sure everyone knows I'm not rolling in the dough, so I don't have to guess what they're going to think. First thing everyone will be avoiding me like the plague.

"Take what you want," Nessa says, reaching into the bag for another handful. "She'll just buy more next week."

Must be nice to have a mother who spoils you to the nines, buying you anything you want and then some. I say, city people have a strange way of spending their money. You wouldn't hear tell of that back in Tanner. Back home candy's a treat, something you maybe get once a week — and that's only if you're lucky. Talk is, being the only girl in the family, Nessa has a mother who bends over backwards to give her all she wants. I say Nessa should count her lucky stars instead of tossing her treats away like they don't mean diddly-squat. If you ask me she's got the mother of all mothers, the mother who only lives in my dreams.

"Have some, Cammie," Nessa says, shaking the candy under my nose. I glance down into the bag, casual-like. Humbugs — if I was to guess. It's been a dog's age since I've had any.

"No thanks," I say, flopping down on my bed like it's no big deal. I'm not giving Nessa the satisfaction of seeing me reach into her paper bag, no matter how much I might be drooling for a taste.

I can sense Nessa standing over me even with my eyes shut. There's nothing worse than knowing you're being gawked at even if you can't see the person doing the gawking. I got my fill of that back in Tanner. Her breath draws in and out about as loud as old man Harvey back home, only he's up in his nineties and had TB when he was young. What's Nessa's excuse?

Keeping my eyes closed, I hope she'll scram. I'm tempted to let out a snotty comment, but I restrain it due to the fact that she's got something on me. I'm not much for tiptoeing around people's feelings. Even though I'm dying to know why she hasn't opened her trap yet, I'm not about to ask. Let sleeping dogs lie, Evelyn Merry would say.

"I was just trying to be nice," she says, kind of huffy.

I open my eyes a teeny crack when I hear her walking away. She goes back to where the other girls are, the paper bag rustling all the way. When Amy and Tammy start squabbling over the humbugs, I jump off the bed and head toward my locker. The door's stuck again so I give it a quick thump with my fist — a trick I learned the other day from Mary Louise; for a pint-sized girl she can sure pack a punch. It pops open.

Evelyn's letter is right on top. Grabbing it up, I head off to find some quiet place for myself. Some things are too precious to share with anyone. Fourteen girls living in the same dormitory, the second someone leaves a fart everyone knows it. The only things in the recreation room are tables and chairs — not a soul to be found. Suits me fine. Sometimes all you need is a little time to roll ideas around in your head. Times like this I miss Evelyn Merry the most. All the letters in the world can't take the place of hearing his voice. No one can hatch a scheme like Evelyn. These days I've got no one to count on but myself. A hard knob swells in my throat until I put my thoughts on other things like that sloop ox of Evelyn's.

A Lefty Frizzell song is playing real low in the background. Lefty and Hank, that's all some of the girls here chatter on about. Aunt Millie always thought Hank Williams was the bee's knees. As soon as one of his songs would come on she'd rush over to the radio and crank it up a notch. Sometimes she'd dance. Always she'd sing. I bet if good old Hank could have seen her in action he'd have busted a gut for sure. I go to turn the music off, but change my mind.

"I Love You in A Thousand Ways" is playing. The song's kind of mushy, but what's honky-tonk music without the mush? Someone's either leaving or loving or dying. It seems to me it's a matter of wanting everyone to be as unhappy as you are. Misery loves to have company, so they say. There's plenty of misery in life without people singing their hearts out over it.

"I hate you in a thousand ways," I sing. Changing the words gives me a smidge of satisfaction as I pretend to sing to Nessa. Carefully, I take Evelyn's letter out. Something inside the envelope catches my eye — a four-leaf clover, dried and pressed. I didn't see it the first time round. I can't help but smile. It never hurts to have luck on your side. Leave it to Evelyn Merry to know what I need. This four-leaf clover might just come in handy. Finding my mother in this big old monster of a city will be as challenging a job as any I've ever done. I'll take all the luck I can get.

Laying my glasses on the table, I hold Evelyn's letter up close to see. Pictures pepper my brain as I read about the day Spark got out of the fence, and how his pa had to round him up. I bet it would be funny to hear Evelyn tell it. Three times I read through the letter, each time adding a little extra to the picture that's already in my head. If I have to be here and Evelyn there, at least he's got that steer he always wanted. A brockle-face one at that. Having seen the brockle-face cow in Jim Merry's pasture makes it a whole lot easier to picture what Spark looks like. Thinking about Evelyn teaching his steer to lead, yelling out "Gee" and "Haw," pulls a smile on my face every time. What I wouldn't give to see that. Most of all I picture his pa standing back watching, maybe even smiling himself because, now that he doesn't drink anymore, he isn't such a bad man after all.

Figuring Nessa's candy is a thing of the past, every last piece gobbled up and swallowed, I mosey on back to the dormitory. The bell's about to ring for bedtime anyway. Going to bed with the chickens is taking some getting used to. Aunt Millie let me stay up as late as I wanted so long as I kept to my room after nine.

As I'm about to pull back the covers on my bed and climb in, I catch sight of something on top of my pillow. I go in for a closer look. Jawbreakers, three of them, round and smooth. Nessa runs on over. I pause, look up to see her smiling like a goon, and scoop the jawbreakers up off my pillow in one slick movement. I climb into bed and roll over. When something comes your way without you having to go bumming for it, I say it's one of those things that was meant to be. No thanks required.

Chapter Eight

Faith can move mountains — that's what Mae Cushion said one day in her store. It was right after me and Evelyn had blown up Hux Wagner's moonshine still and Evelyn landed in the hospital. Even Aunt Millie nodded her head that day, and her agreeing with Mae was as unlikely as her throwing her arms up into the air and praising God in all his glory — an honest-to-goodness miracle by my calculation. While I didn't see any mountains being moved when Evelyn was in the hospital, I knew faith had to be powerful. Evelyn got to go home when most everyone said he wouldn't, and that's all I care about.

Thinking about what Mae Cushion had to say about faith moving mountains, I make my way down to the dining room in the middle of the night. The school puts plenty of faith in us, expecting we'll stay in our beds all night long. But I've got a bit of news for them — they've never come up against a Turple before.

My stomach is having a spree for itself, rumbling and thrashing about. It'll probably wake up everyone in the dorm. I pop the last jawbreaker Nessa left on my pillow into my mouth. No wonder I'm having trouble falling asleep. Before chasing me off to bed, Aunt Millie would spread me some bread and honey. The gang sitting around the kitchen would stop talking and watch. I used to think they were jealous, me with bread and honey when all they had was some of Hux's moonshine to drink, until the night Aunt Millie barked out at them, "Cammie isn't some circus sideshow. Now drink up." A jawbreaker isn't going to fill the empty spot in my stomach. What I wouldn't give for a piece of Aunt Millie's homemade bread and honey right about now.

There's always a bit of light in the hallway at night here. Nighttime comes and my mind gets the wandering fever. The strangest thoughts won't get out of my head, like me wondering what Aunt Millie's really up to or imagining Evelyn leading Spark around the dooryard. Does Miss Muise miss me being in school back in Tanner? Once you've tossed and turned in your bed enough times there's no way possible to settle down for a good sleep. Until now I haven't got up the courage to go exploring on my own. It's easy to get to the dining room when you're following the supervisor.

Realizing that no one checks in on us after lights out, my mind's been conjuring ways to get out of here and find my mother. Even if I was able to sneak out in the middle of the night, I'd have no idea how to go about finding Burnham Street. It's not like you can go knocking on doors after midnight. Sneaking off to the dining room is one thing; Burnham Street is a whole other story.

The sweetness from the jawbreakers haunts the inside of my mouth as I tiptoe along. The thought about sneaking down to the dining room wormed into my head as I lay in bed rolling one of the jawbreakers around in my mouth. Waiting for everyone to stop cackling and start sleeping took forever. I couldn't risk telling anyone what I had up my sleeve. Hard to say who can be trusted around this joint. I could tell anything to Evelyn Merry. They'd have had to take a crowbar to pry his lips open. When it comes to keeping secrets, Evelyn's a real crackerjack. I don't much expect these nattering girls to hold my secrets anytime soon. I'm waiting for Nessa to let the cat out of the bag to prove that point.

I'm still getting a feel for things here. Everyone seems friendly enough, but who's to know? Hal Perry seemed friendly, too, until he grabbed me on my way to the outhouse one night in the dark. Aunt Millie came running, put him in his place right smartly, and told him to never come back. That was the one and only time she told someone to hit the road and actually stuck with it.

My insides make a mountain-size rumble. Maybe I should go back to bed, wait out the hunger, hopefully fall asleep without having another crazy dream with Aunt Millie in it. That thought lasts about as long as a snowball in a pot of boiling water. I keep on going. I don't have much choice, seeing as how I'm about to faint away from hunger right here on the spot.

I step through the doorway with caution. The dining room feels spooky in the quiet of night. When you've got bad eyes, things don't always make sense in the daylight, let alone at night. Some things you can decipher in your head without giving it too much thought — everyday things like tables and chairs. I'm pretty good at putting two and two together, figuring out what those blurry images are in the distance. But when it's something I've never seen before, that's a whole other story.

Running my hands along the counter, I hope to find some food that hasn't been put away. I root through the cupboards. Nothing. Not a speck. I reach above me, feeling all around, careful not to make a thump when I close the doors. Just as I'm chewing over the fact that an ant would starve to death in this place, I strike gold. A loaf of bread, an entire loaf, not a slice taken off! I hold it like a baby in my arms. Thinking that I'll never find a lick of honey to spread on it, I catch of whiff of peanut butter in the air. Spinning around on my heels, I'm about ready to spring a leak when someone whispers, "Want something to put on that bread?"

Gasping and jumping at the same time, I manage to sputter out, "How did you? Where did you?" I didn't even know I was being followed.

Nessa laughs. "I brought the peanut butter from home. When it comes to late-night snacking, you're looking at a professional here. Now all we need is a knife."

Thinking it's mighty bold of her to assume I'll share my bread, I start rooting through the drawers. It's not like we're the best of friends, ready to share fifty-fifty the way me and Evelyn always did. We're not friends, period. To top it all off, she didn't even ask in a nice way. *Finders keepers, losers weepers* I want to cry, but have a quick change of heart. Bread with nothing to spread on it will make a mighty dry lunch. It's one of those cutting-off-your-nose-to-spite-your-face moments people talk about. Someone else, I wouldn't give it a second thought. I'd be more than happy to share. But Nessa Maxwell — why is she always showing up in my space?

The next grumble my stomach makes is loud as the cannon fire from Citadel Hill — or at least enough to wake up the dead. Nessa giggles. The view might be pretty sweet up here on my high horse, but it isn't going to fill the empty spot in my belly. Sometimes you've got to give in for your own good. I could tell Nessa this doesn't mean a thing. She's still a bigmouth and a show-off. Accepting that all that isn't going to change any time soon, I hand her a table knife. Nessa grabs it like this is going to be her last meal on this earth.

"We haven't got all night," she says when I let a grunt out of me.

I send her a stinkeye for being all grabby and bossy before tearing into the loaf with both hands. Time's a-wasting. I pull off two big hunks. A quick dip into peanut butter and Nessa brings up enough for two. She smears some on both pieces of bread. Like a couple of pigs smacking their way through a pail of slop, we don't stop until the loaf is half gone.

With my stomach ready to burst at the seams, I hold up the loaf and ask Nessa if she wants the rest. She takes it from me.

"It might come in handy again," she says, putting it back in the bag. In the dim light of the dining room I can barely make out her wide-mouthed grin. She hides what's left of the bread at the back of the cupboard — the jar of peanut butter, too. Her statement about being a professional late-night snacker sure wasn't an exaggeration.

Before we leave I try to set her straight. Let her know that just because we shared some grub it doesn't mean this is the start of any friendship between us. Just a matter of being in the same place at the same time — me with a loaf of bread, her with a jar of peanut butter. Nothing else.

She whips around and I tap her on the shoulder. "Listen, Nessa, this doesn't mean anything —"

She cuts me off with a, "Ssh! Someone's coming."

No one's coming. This is just bait to shut me up. I can see through that. I still don't trust her the length of my nose. She knows my deepest secret, the one I've been holding in my heart since I was old enough to remember. And it's not as if I shared the information of my own free will. She snuck up and stole it out from under me when I wasn't looking.

"This isn't funny, Nessa," I protest. Her hand clamps down across my mouth. For a moment the flames are burning in me. Seconds before I sink my teeth into her palm, I hear someone walk into the dining room.

"Who's in here?" We jump at the sound of Miss Turner's voice. That fire of anger quickly snuffs itself out as Nessa loosens her hand from my face. Like cornered snakes twisted into a little ball in the corner, there's no place for us to slither away to. My mind buzzes. What will our punishment be?

"Close your eyes," whispers Nessa.

"But —"

"Just do what I say." She nudges me with her elbow. I have no choice.

"It's Cammie, Miss Turner! She was sleepwalking. I tried to stop her."

My arms shoot out in front of me. Not that I'm an authority when it comes to sleepwalking, but I've heard a thing or two. My heart's drumming like partridge wings as I wait to see what Miss Turner will say. I pull in a quick breath. The footsteps are close. The light comes on.

Disbelief skids across her tongue as she croaks out, "Sleepwalking?" I have my ideas that she's sharp enough to see right through that excuse — not like the music teacher, Mrs. Fenwick, who'd believe you if you said you'd been to Mars and back — but she doesn't let on. Then again, Miss Turner has the reputation of being a pushover when it comes to enforcing the rules. The girls don't seem too concerned when she's on duty.

"I followed Cammie down. I'm sure glad you showed up, Miss Turner. I didn't know what to do," says Nessa pulling off the performance of a lifetime. "You're not supposed to wake someone who's sleepwalking. They'll die from fright if you do. And I didn't want to be responsible for that. I get in enough trouble as it is."

"Die from fright? I don't know that I've ever heard that before," says Miss Turner, doubt now step-dancing all around the dining room. It slides right over to where we're standing, trying to catch us in a big whopper of a lie. Miss Turner clomps toward us and stops directly in front of me. My heart works overtime as I wait to see if she'll buy Nessa's story.

"Let's get her back to bed," she says, taking me by the arm. Grabbing the opportunity, I spring my eyelids open and flutter them a few times.

"Where am I?" I ask, looking around as if in a stupor. When you're running the rig on someone you've got to add all those little details to make yourself be believed. Nessa isn't the only one who can act.

"You're in the dining room," answers Miss Turner with a queer little sound in her voice.

"The dining room? How did I get here?" I twist my head around from side to side real quick so as to show my surprise at discovering where I am.

"You walked here, silly — in your sleep," Nessa slaps me on the back as she laughs. Her acting abilities are almost better than Aunt Millie's. Even I would believe her.

"Off to bed with you both," says Miss Turner, sounding about as stern as a mewing kitten. As Nessa grasps my hand, pure relief blows through me like a whistling wind.

We don't even trade whispers on our way back to the dormitory. We got ourselves out of one scrape; next time

I might not be so lucky. One thing I know, if I'm going to find a way to fly the coop, I'll have to make it a foolproof plan, one that won't backfire on me the way this did. I'll only get one chance to make a break for it — after that they'll be watching me like a hawk.

"I smell peanut butter," comes a murmur in the dark just as I'm about to snuggle down under the covers. Sitting up in bed, I whisper a quick thank you into the air. If it reaches as far as Nessa's bed, then so be it. Let the dust settle where it may, as Aunt Millie likes to say.

"You're welcome," comes a muffled reply.

Maybe Nessa isn't all *that* bad. She could have squealed on me to save her own skin, and that has to say something decent about her. I suppose sometimes you've got to step down off that high horse no matter how grand the view might be.

Chapter Nine

Like blackflies in the springtime, the smell of fresh lilacs swarms the air. I look up from the checkerboard at the pretty blue dress coming toward us.

"Don't look now, but here comes Miss Turner," I whisper to Nessa, whose back is to the doorway. It's not hard to recognize Miss Turner from a distance. I've already figured out her walk and the smell of her perfume. She also wears blue a lot — my favourite colour. Everyone's got their own style, their own way of carrying themselves in the world. It's not hard to figure out if you pay attention.

While Nessa slides her red checker to the next square, Miss Turner zeroes in on us. I brace myself for what might be coming — a reminder of our antics from the other night being first and foremost. I'm pretty sure Miss Turner smelled the peanut butter on us. I've been a little skittish of her the last couple of days, wondering if she's going to bring the whole matter up. It might not be too late for her to report the incident to Mr. Allen.

"No more sleepwalking, Cammie?" she asks, stopping beside our table. First moving my checker, I look up and start off with a cheery, "Nice to see you, Miss Turner," before adding an, "If I *have* been out roaming around, I'd be the last to know." I finish it all off with a big smile. You've got to hand out the pleasantries when you're trying to keep on someone's good side. The last thing I need is to land myself in trouble. I haven't been around here long enough to have grown on anyone. They might send me packing without ever knowing who I really am as a person. I've got some good ways about me (back home, Miss Muise liked to say I was the model student), but no one's had time to see me in action.

"I can vouch for her," chirps Nessa. "She's been sleeping like a log." Not that things are all hunky-dory between me and Nessa, but being sociable with her might be in my best interest. Nessa's got connections. You never know when those connections could work in my favour. Then there's that other business she's got hanging over me.

"I have a feeling you'd be the one to know, Vanessa. Cammie's lucky to have you for a shadow — especially a nighttime shadow. When I was a girl I'd go open the front door in my sleep. Mum would catch me staring at the night sky and take me back to bed." We chuckle along with Miss Turner. People like to think their stories are something to be tittered about.

Nessa studies the board for a few seconds and jumps my checker, scooping up my last king like an expert. I've been skunked again.

"Are you looking to take Nessa on?" I say.

Miss Turner is standing over us, scrutinizing the board. The quicker I get her off the subject of sleepwalking, the better. Plus, I can't be guaranteed that Nessa won't sing like a canary if she gets caught off guard.

"I'm not sure, Cammie. I hear Vanessa's the champ — nearly unbeatable."

Nessa must be on top of the world with all that praise coming her way. Hands down, she's the best player in the dormitory, and she's been on a roll this past while. The checkers line up in her favour, like they know what her next move is going to be before she makes it. Having just learned to play a few days ago, I'm not looking to beat Nessa any time soon. Maybe Miss Turner will have better luck.

"I've won a *few* games," says Nessa. I can't imagine her saying that without exploding inside, but Nessa doesn't even crack a grin.

"She *is* good, but eventually everyone gets tossed to the crows. This might be your lucky day, Miss Turner."

Jumping out of my seat, I take Miss Turner's hand, warm as toast, and pull her down into the chair. When she giggles, the loose blonde curls on top of her head bounce. A few weeks back she got a home permanent put in. I overheard the maids raving about it one day, how it was just as good as you'd get at the hairdresser's. I've got to admit it does look quite spiffy. A twinge of envy strikes me. The hair I arrived with now looks like it was gnawed off by a mouse thanks to the scissor-happy barber who's only ever cut hair in the army. They say he comes back every few months, so I guess growing long hair is out of the question.

"Far be it from me to toss anyone to the crows," says Miss Turner, already lining her checkers up. She shakes out her hands, getting herself ready. "I'll warn you, though. Growing up I played a lot of checkers. Of course, it's been ages ago now," she says, taking the first move. Nessa quickly counters. A few smooth moves on the board and Miss Turner skips over two of Nessa's checkers all in one smash, stacking them up beside her right elbow.

"I did warn you," she says apologetically.

That seems to have knocked the confidence out of Nessa. She inspects the board, getting in closer than she needs to. I let out a sigh as Nessa dances her checker back and forth between two squares, trying to anticipate Miss

Turner's next move. I tell Nessa to take it easy. It's just a silly game.

The moment Nessa jumps one of Miss Turner's checkers, her smile looks about ready to split her face in half. When she makes another jump right afterward I become suspicious. Maybe Miss Turner is taking pity on her, letting her get the upper hand for a time. Three jumps later and that theory gets shot down. Miss Turner is cleaning up, closing in on her — getting ready for the kill. She takes off her glasses, wipes them with a hanky before putting them back on her face. She's unstoppable.

Nessa lets out a sigh and leans her head against her elbow, not looking the least bit interested in the game now that Miss Turner's winning.

"Take that sour look off your face, Nessa," I say, trying to lighten the mood. "You remind me of Cyrus Wilkes back home in Tanner, playing checkers down at Mae Cushion's store on Saturday afternoon." Unfortunately, my idea backfires and no one laughs.

"I used to know someone from Tanner," Miss Turner says, her eyes glued on Nessa's next move.

"Hey! Maybe it's someone I know." Imagine running across someone who's heard of that little dot on the map. I'm curious and just happy to hear that someone from the city actually has something in common with me, Cammie Turple.

"Never kick a horse turd, it might be your uncle," Ed likes to say whenever some coincidence brings you face to face with some long-lost cousin a hundred times removed. His point being, you just never know if you'll come across some stranger who is either related to or else knows someone you do.

"Oh, I doubt that. All she talked about was getting as far away from Tanner as possible. She had some pretty big plans." Miss Turner's voice flows like maple syrup. She looks up from the board and smiles like she's thinking about something — like maybe that person she once knew from Tanner.

"What was her name?" If Miss Turner doesn't soon tell I'll bust open with curiosity. It's not like I know everyone who ever lived in Tanner, but wouldn't it be the oddest coincidence if it was someone I've heard tell of.

"Millie — her name was Millie."

"My aunt's name is Millie!" I say as loud as any hallelujah has ever been shouted. Good old Ed was right. Imagine finding a horse turd here in my brand-new life, miles and miles away from home. I'm feeling pretty pleased until common sense pokes my shoulder: if Miss Turner knows Aunt Millie from all those years ago, she'd know about her business dealings. I quickly rethink my earlier enthusiasm. Even someone as nice as Miss Turner would have a hard time accepting me once she found out who my aunt is.

I have no plans to decipher whether or not this is a possibility. If the word gets out that my aunt was a bootlegger, my name will be toast. I'll be a laughingstock here just like back home in Tanner. Only I won't be Blind-Eyed Cammie, I'll be Bootleg Cammie Turple. Who will care that Aunt Millie's a *reformed* bootlegger?

Miss Turner's voice sounds strained as she squeezes out, "Margaret." She gives a strange little laugh. "Oh, listen to me — her name wasn't Millie at all. It was Margaret...Margaret something or other." She gives another queer laugh. "And here I've always prided myself with having a good memory...Have you ever heard tell of any Margarets in Tanner?"

"Nope. No Margarets in Tanner." What a relief! Glad that got straightened out. Besides, it doesn't make sense that someone like Miss Turner would be friends with Aunt Millie. One thing's for certain, I've got to watch myself. This is a lesson for me. I can't be saying things without using my brain first.

Miss Turner cleans the last of Nessa's checkers up off the board. She smiles and says it was fun but now she's got to get going. Her seat doesn't have time to cool off before I plunk myself down. I line up the checkers for another game, quickly taking the first move. In true Nessa style, she counters my move.

"What's *her* problem?" Nessa asks as soon as we hear Miss Turner's shoes scuffing down the hallway. Two quick moves later, she's made her first jump. She makes it look so easy.

"Problem?" I say, scooping a checker off the board. Satisfaction marches through me. I might just win this time.

"She was acting all strange when you told her your aunt's name. Did you see the look on her face?" Nessa starts to move her checker, then slides it back.

"I didn't see anything." Nessa heard me in the bathroom. She knows Aunt Millie's a bootlegger. I'm willing to bet she hasn't forgotten that tidbit. "Maybe she was embarrassed," I add. "She probably felt dumb mixing up Millie and Margaret like that." I wait for Nessa to make another move, hoping she'll get off the subject of Aunt Millie. Pronto.

"Maybe…" It's impossible not to miss the hesitation in Nessa's voice. Still, I pretend not to catch on to what she's insinuating.

"I think we might have a mystery on our hands," says Nessa just then.

"A mystery? Oh, Nessa, there you go, making mountains out of molehills." This time *I* make the queer laugh.

Sometimes you've got to play dumb in life. There are times when being your own smart self will only make more problems than it solves.

Chapter Ten

The chain-link fence separating the boys' playground from the girls' is chilly. I shake out my hand and blow on my fingers. I'm taking a chance just being here at recess, but things don't happen unless you're willing to take a risk from time to time. The leaves surround the playground, forming a patchwork of red and orange and yellow. A few trickle to the ground in the breeze. Already it's the middle of October and I haven't worked up the courage to ask for help getting to Burnham Street. Since I'm lacking in the note-tossing department, another line of action seemed in order. Last night thoughts came raining down on me as I pitched about in bed. Plans shift and change. You've got to be flexible. I'm a rubber band. I've got to be if I intend to get to where I want to go.

The boys are yelping in play, making quick zigzags back and forth like ants at a picnic; others are huddling near the far side of the fence. What's a person got to do to get a little attention around here? Am I invisible or something? At this rate it'll take an entire school year to talk to a boy, let alone work up the courage to ask one of them for help. You can't expect someone you hardly know to do you a favour of this magnitude. Friendships take time to build.

Cries from behind me of "Red Rover, Red Rover, we call Nessa on over," tantalize the heck out of me. Red Rover is one of my favourite games. I hold my ground. The Turple in me won't give in.

I'm a little on edge standing here by the fence all by myself, a sitting duck of the highest degree. I expected the boys would see me standing by the fence and head on over. A lot I know. I take a few steps back. I don't want to arouse the supervisor's attention. You never know when one of them will show up.

Nessa's voice rings out across the playground. She's calling my name and I spin around. Hurrying toward the line of girls with their hands locked, I see an opening and I take it. A hand on either side of me squeezes mine. A voice calls out, "Red Rover, Red Rover, we call Cammie on over." Releasing the hands I'm holding fast to, I race across the playground smiling. I'm not invisible. Not anymore.

When lunchtime swings around I've decided this plan to find my mother is going to require further consideration.

There has to be a way to get acquainted with the boys other than waiting for the Christmas dance in December. Could be one of the boys likes the sound of my voice. Myself, I'm kind of partial to Barry Huphman's. His soft way of speaking kind of reminds me of Evelyn Merry. And he saved my skin in Mrs. Christi's class the other week. That counts for a lot. But right now he's just a voice, since I can't even get close enough to tell what colour his hair is.

Once classes are over for the day, Mrs. Galloway hands out the mail in the supervisor's lounge and there's a letter for me. I flip it over and check the return address: Aunt Millie. A shock wave ripples through me. Letters have come from Evelyn every couple of weeks and I even got one from Miss Muise, but I never in a million years expected to get anything from Aunt Millie. I put it in my locker to read later. I'm not even sure I want to.

Most everyone gets mail. When a parcel arrives from Newfoundland or Prince Edward Island you'd swear Christmas arrived early. Having the other girls brag about the parcels they get sometimes leaves me wishing Aunt Millie would wrap up a little something and send it off. It's not like a few penny candies every now and again would hurt her. But, like everything involving Aunt Millie, it usually comes down to her not having a thoughtful bone in her body. If I want candy, Nessa would be more than happy to share. Most times I don't take any when she offers it. It isn't about the candy. It never will be. Believe it or not, I've got principles. You can't always be taking from someone without giving something back in return. Besides, she could have something up her sleeve. This nice act of hers could be just that — an act. You wouldn't need to be too bright to figure that one out.

Curiosity finally gets to me.

Opening the envelope feels a little strange, seeing Aunt Millie's handwriting on the page. Taking my glasses off, I hold it up close and read the *Dear Cammie* part. I squirm a bit on the edge of the bed — things are likely to get nasty from here on out. I can feel it in my bones.

Dear Cammie,
Since I already warned you about Ed, and you didn't seem to want to listen, I have more I want to add to what I told you on the telephone the other week. It would be in your best interest to keep reading and not just ball this up and toss it away.

I let out a grunt. It's like she can read my mind.

Ed might mean well, but he really hasn't a clue as to what he's doing, coming up with some lame idea of adopting you now that he's got a lady friend in his life. The world is filled with people meaning to do well, but in the end they just ruin the lives of others.

Ed ruined your mother's life. It's why she took off the way she did. I've never told you this before, mainly because I didn't want you to think Ed was a schmuck, but the real reason he never married your mother didn't have a thing to do with him going off to war. Back then Ed was even more irresponsible than he is now, if you can believe that. He was charming, though, and Brenda fell under his spell. She was young and Ed was her first love — puppy love, really. I told her but she wouldn't listen.

I never wanted to be the one to say, "I told you so," but I was right about Brenda and Ed all along. In the end Brenda told me she couldn't stand Ed's recklessness, and the way he'd take off right out of the blue when something struck his fancy. Brenda was a serious young girl with big plans of getting married and having a family one day. I promised Brenda I wouldn't ever tell you any of this because she never believed in badmouthing another human being, even one who did her wrong. Brenda's a lot more generous than I am.

Ed's backing me into a corner right now and I've got no choice but to lay the truth down at your feet. You're a big girl and it's high time you knew the real facts. Ed was the one who broke it off with Brenda. Ran off with her best friend is what he did. And he broke her heart, pure and simple. Ed's *not a bad man, I've never said he was, but if the past is any indication of the future I can't just let you go off with him. No matter what Ed thinks, he won't be adopting you. You're mine — at least until Brenda comes for you. I'm signing off now. I've had my say.*

Signed,
Aunt Millie

Badmouthing Ed must be Aunt Millie's new pastime. But the truth is, part of me doesn't mind the letter so much. Reading about the way my parents met gives me something to hold fast to. It might not be some fancy fairy tale, but at least it's my life. Yet something about all this still doesn't make sense. Aunt Millie has her drawers in a knot over this adoption thing — but why? It's not like much would change, except maybe I'd be going off to stay with Ed over the summer and Christmas vacation. Being away at school, my time spent with Aunt Millie is pretty skimpy anyway.

I put my glasses back on. You'd think Aunt Millie had some say in the matter of this adoption. *At least until Brenda comes for you.* I let out a grunt. I squeeze the letter tight in my fist before putting it away in my locker. Hearing that same old song, year after year, gets mighty tiresome to the ears.

Chapter Eleven

Flopping down on my bunk, I reach for the envelope I've got hidden under my mattress. The stampede's over. Everyone's down in the recreation room, waiting for *The Sealed Book* to come on. The minute that big gong sounds they all suck in air. That's when the keeper of the book opens the door to the vault and it's like you're hearing it all first hand, the creeks, thumps, and whistling wind coming over the airwaves. A fright shimmies up my spine every single time — stories of murder, mystery, and dark deeds. I can't admit all those eerie sounds give me the willies. Maybe this time I'll pass. Before I can haul the envelope out I realize there's someone standing beside my bed.

"I've been thinking — you're the one who wrote that note in Mrs. Christi's class, aren't you?"

Nessa Maxwell. I've been trying to be decent to her without getting too chummy. I sit up quickly, swinging my legs over the side of the bed.

"Come on! It's almost time for *The Sealed Book*." I jump to my feet. Just as I'm about to make my getaway, Nessa grabs me by the arm.

"You're hiding something," she says. "But I haven't figured out what. Does this have something to do with your mother?"

There. Finally. I knew it was too good to be true, Nessa keeping her trap shut all these weeks. I break loose from her grip and spin around.

"What will it take for your silence? I'll do whatever you want. Just name it," I say, feeling suddenly brave. I might just as well find out what she wants.

"Keep me quiet?" she says, making a face.

"Don't play dumb with me. You know my secrets. Who all did you tell?" I'm through playing nice just to keep Nessa quiet. Sometimes you've got to jump in with both feet.

"I'm not a squealer, if that's what you mean," says Nessa. "If I was going to say something about what I heard, don't you think I would have by now?"

I roll this idea around for a bit, feel it slowly dissolve like a jawbreaker on my tongue. It's not like she's tried to blackmail me or anything.

"Is it so hard to believe I just want to be friends?"

Something in Nessa's voice finally gets to me as we stand there in the empty dorm. She's right. All this time and she hasn't made a peep. Call me gullible, but I believe her. The weight on my shoulders is suddenly gone. Sometimes you've got to put your trust in someone even if you're not sure you want to. Seizing the moment, I smile real big and say, "I don't suppose you can take me to Burnham Street."

"Burnham Street? That's no problem...we'll just call a cab. I do it all the time when I'm at my grandmother's house."

A cab. I never would have thought of that. I can see that being friends with Nessa will have its advantages. Sometimes you just don't see the things that are right under your nose. Nessa knows all the buildings and streets here. Halifax *is* her home, after all.

For a second I'm on cloud nine. At last I'm going to get to where I want to go, but then my hopes suddenly spiral to the ground. "I don't have money to pay for a cab," I groan.

A grin spreads across Nessa's face. "Maybe you don't... but I do."

"I can't let you do that," I say, my head hanging low. Accepting the occasional candy from Nessa is one thing, but letting her pay out money for a cab? I don't think so.

"Look, it'll only cost a few dollars, anyway."

"A few dollars I don't have." I guess people who have money don't know what it's like to be broke.

"Don't worry about it. You can pay me back later." While that sounds good, it's not very realistic. I shake my head. Money doesn't grow on trees.

"Look, you can get a job here washing dishes when you turn twelve," says Nessa. "You can pay me then."

A job? How come I've never heard about this before? I know some of the older girls help out in the dining room, but I had no idea they get paid. I'm as hard a worker as the next person. All those years helping out in Aunt Millie's kitchen didn't hurt none, either. With this new bit of information tucked away, I finally say, "Are you sure about this?"

"I'm positive."

"Oh, and it's Miss Turner's weekend on duty," I remind her.

"I'll call my mother and tell her I'm going to stay all weekend. She won't care. And one more thing — we'll need a diversion," says Nessa, hardly missing a beat. A devious smile spreads across her face. I've seen that same conniving look on Evelyn Merry's face when he's cooking something up.

"A diversion — what kind of diversion?" Listen to me, sounding so unsure. You'd swear I didn't know a thing myself about concocting a plan.

"Just leave it to me," says Nessa. "It'll be a piece of cake."

—

Saturday comes and I can scarcely sit still during morning classes. Dinner in the dining room and my stomach isn't interested. I pick at the corned beef and cabbage on my plate, forcing myself to chew and swallow. Nessa's as cool as a cucumber, talking and laughing like we aren't a few hours away from breaking out of here. I don't know how she can be so calm. Stealing out of here without being discovered won't be as easy as sneaking out of Aunt Millie's house to go meet up with Evelyn Merry. Hard to escape a place when your every move is under scrutiny.

When two o'clock comes, things swing into action. I grab Nessa's hand and we hurry toward the lobby.

"Slow down, girls. It isn't a race," says Miss Turner, sweet as a strawberry tart fresh out of the oven.

"Nessa has to make a call," I say, yanking on Nessa's arm.

"She's such a pushover," whispers Nessa, hardly slowing our pace. Seems kind of mean, us taking advantage of Miss Turner's good nature this way, but when you're working at being devious, you've got to stack all the cards in your favour. We won't have much time to track down my mother, but going by car will sure speed things up. It'll be tricky, but not impossible.

The lobby is deserted. Freedom is just beyond the front doors. So close I could taste it if I stuck out my tongue. But get caught sticking your tongue out here and you could be high-stepping it to Mr. Allen's office with a lecture about "behaving in a ladylike fashion."

"Who's on duty today?" I ask, knowing that one of the older boys is usually in charge of ringing the bell in the lobby. I could be envious of all that Nessa can see if I stopped to think about it. Not that her eyesight's perfect, but it's a lot better than mine. When Nessa says she's sure it's Allison Gillis, I bite my lip to keep a bad word from slipping out. Allison's one of the senior boys, and he has a reputation for being a stickler for the rules. All happy, it would seem, being the boss when it's time to ring the bell for bedtime or mealtime or just changing classes. It wouldn't surprise me if he ends up being a prison warden when he grows up.

"Hi, Allison," Nessa calls out, arm waving in the air as we breeze past. "We're just using the telephone." We march up to the pay station, big as you please. I can hardly believe our brazen selves. Nessa thumbs through the telephone directory, finally running her finger down one of the pages as she looks for the name of a cab company. Good thing one of us knows what she's doing. So far, I'm just along for the ride.

"Dependable Cab sounds good to me," says Nessa all snappy-like.

I have to agree. It sounds so, I don't know, dependable. If you can't depend upon the Dependable Cab Company, there's surely something wrong with the world.

Nessa repeats the number a few times until it's imprinted in her memory. When someone marches across the lobby, she snaps the telephone book shut. As the clicking of shoes gets farther away, she drops a nickel into the pay phone and starts dialling. *The suspense is killing me.* What will she say? Me, I'd be stumbling all over my words, afraid of being found out. But not cool-as-a-cucumber Nessa Maxwell. This girl knows what she's doing.

"Hello." Nessa adds a twang to her voice to make herself sound older. "Yes. I'd like a cab."

Simple yet to the point — certainly not overdone. I giggle into my hand as I wonder if we'll actually get away with this. I'm dying to know what's being said on the other end of that telephone line.

"Where am I calling from? University Street. The Halifax School for the Blind. Yes…I said, 'for the blind.'" Nessa puckers up her face. I push my fist into my mouth, trying to keep any noise from escaping.

"I want to go to Burnham Street, but I haven't got a lot of time. I've got someone to find, only I'm not sure where on Burnham Street she is." I cringe. Nessa's letting her tongue waggle. *Loose lips sink ships*, Aunt Millie likes to say. I give Nessa a quick jab in the ribs. She looks at me and makes a face. "Yes. Yes…I'm real busy today, so can you come in half an hour?" I look up and down the hallway. The coast is still clear. The bird inside my chest is flapping away as Nessa signs off.

"Phase one." Nessa shows her big white teeth and sounds pleased. "So far, so good. Now for phase two — the diversion."

Now that we got past this first step of ours, I make a quick nod. The kind of nod that fills you with confidence much better than a lazy one ever could. I need to have all the confidence I can if this plan of ours is going to work.

Chapter Twelve

We beat it up to the dormitory to prepare for phase two. On our way there the worry worms starts to crawl.

"We should have told the taxi driver to come to the back of the school."

Nessa gives me that same look Aunt Millie used to, the one that seemed to say, "Quiet down, knucklehead." I clam up pretty quick. My two cents aren't worth much at this point. If I've learned anything from being around Aunt Millie, it's when to keep my mouth shut.

It didn't take much coaxing on our part to persuade Jennie and Amy to help. A few handfuls of Nessa's candy and they'd agree to just about anything (the same way Aunt Millie could get Fred Donner to fill up her woodbox with a drink of moonshine when it was calling for a storm).

Ten minutes before the cab is due to arrive, the four of us casually head out of the dorm. At the top of the stairs,

Nessa gives Amy and Jennie some last-minute instructions. When you're carrying out a top-secret mission, everyone can use a little coaching.

"Remember, Amy, once Jennie fakes her fit you've got to keep Allison occupied long enough for us to slip out the front door. And Jennie, twist and turn, do whatever you have to. Make it look believable. The worst fit you've ever had. " It's been a while since Jennie's last seizure — by now everyone's come to expect them. Still, it disrupts the class. You can't just leave someone wiggling on the floor.

"What are you two *really* up to, anyway?" asks Amy, handing down her curiosity like we've got time for any of this. I stick my face in close to hers.

"What you don't know won't hurt you," I rattle off in my toughest voice. But Amy's not satisfied. She's got this habit of wringing her hands when she's nervous. I first noticed it the night of the séance, the way she was fiddling and twisting her fingers when Miss Turner showed up on the scene.

"Just do what we say and don't ask questions," says Nessa, finishing it off with a, "Or you'll be sorry!" that finally puts the lid on Amy's nosiness. Easy to see who's got clout around here. Amy's not about to run the risk of crossing Nessa — even I know that.

"What if they figure out I'm faking?" Jennie whimpers like a lost pup. I sigh. I thought we'd been through this about twenty times already. We definitely don't have time for this, but I don't want to get snotty with Jennie, seeing how she's the key instrument in our scheme.

"You'll do fine," I say, patting her hand. "I know you will."

"I hope you're right," she says in a pinched voice. I start to wonder if we can pull this off without a hitch. It seems to be getting more complicated by the minute.

"Okay, the coast is clear," says Nessa, giving Amy a gentle shove. "Now go."

A small bleat escapes Jennie when Amy takes her hand. The little bird in my chest is beating its wings —*please don't let Jennie back out at the last moment.*

"As soon as Jennie's on the floor we'll head for the door," I whisper to Nessa, like that hadn't been our plan all along. If Nessa is at all worried, there's no sign of it. My heart makes a hiccough. I draw in a few deep breaths. This is nothing compared to what Evelyn and me used to do back home, so why the nerves?

The thump that follows sounds almost as loud as the time Jeff Nickerson fell out of his chair in Aunt Millie's kitchen one Saturday night. Amy cries out for someone to help and Allison says he'll go for a nurse. Nessa and I head for the front door as Amy continues to call out for help. Something in Amy's voice raises an alarm in me. Either Jennie's putting on the show of the century or else she's not faking. Stopping dead in my tracks, I let go of Nessa's hand.

Nessa whispers, "Come on!" and grabs my hand again. The front door isn't that far away. My legs go stiff. I wasn't expecting to hear Jennie hit the floor that hard. It was louder than the night we had the séance — and that was for real. I push my feet into the floor, holding back.

Amy lets out a "Hurry, Allison!" that would curdle milk, and before you know it the lobby's humming with people and we have ourselves a full-blown racket taking place.

"We can't go," I say. "Not now. Something's wrong." The words catch in my throat. Our plan isn't going to work.

"Come on," coaxes Nessa. "Jennie's just acting. We talked about this. The cab's outside waiting."

I know Nessa's right. There's still time for us to make our escape. No one would even know we were gone. A few minutes from now and I could be standing face to face with mother dearest. We start toward the door, but then I suddenly stop. I can't leave Jennie any more than I could leave Evelyn Merry that day by the river when our plan to blow up Hux's moonshine still backfired on us. Sometimes you've got to let your own wants fall to the wayside. Some things are more important. Nessa pulls on my arm, telling me to hurry. Shaking her off, I turn and run back toward Jennie.

Amidst the commotion a man's voice calls out, "Taxi! Someone called for a taxi. I've been waiting out front. Time is money. I can't wait around all day."

A bit of mumbling follows, but no one answers the driver.

"Our goose is cooked," I whisper to Nessa.

"Look here, someone called for a cab." By now, the taxi driver sounds miffed. He shifts the hat on his head.

"Can't you see we have a medical emergency here?" snaps one of the maids.

By this time, Jennie is slowly being helped to her feet.

"Take her to the sick ward. I'd better call for the doctor. That's quite a bump," says the nurse.

"Taxi!" repeats the driver.

Mrs. Skinner marches over to the taxi driver. "Are you certain someone from here called for a taxi? I can't imagine who," she says, sounding annoyed.

"Look, lady, do you think I'd be here if someone hadn't called for a ride? The call came in about a half hour ago — said they wanted to go to Burnham Street." I'm about ready to scramble for my life, but taking off like a streak of greased lightning will only make me look guilty as sin.

"Burnham Street?"

"That's what I said."

"Did you call for a taxi, Beth?" asks Mrs. Skinner.

"I only take a taxi home when it's raining, otherwise I walk," says Miss Turner.

"That's what I thought. No one else here lives on Burnham Street. And no one from the school would have called for a taxi. There has to be some mix-up," says Mrs. Skinner.

"If no one here wants a taxi, I'm out of here." He stomps across the lobby and slams the door behind him.

Climbing the stairs with Nessa and Amy, I feel like a crumb. This is all my fault, just like last summer when Evelyn got hurt. Me, putting all this time and effort into tracking down a woman who doesn't even care that I exist. And me, involving other people in something that has nothing to do with them. And of all the strange coincidences, turns out Miss Turner lives on Burnham Street — what are the odds of that? I let out a grunt.

—

Later, one of the maids brings Jennie back to the dormitory. There's a knob on her forehead the size of an egg. A badly bruised egg, that is. Nessa passes out the penny candy without being asked. We're all quiet. I go to my locker and give it a whack with my fist. The door swings open. I root around until I find the letter I'm writing to Evelyn. I was thinking I'd finish it off by telling him about this afternoon's antics, but I decide against it. All that will accomplish is making Nessa and I look like we can't pull off a simple plan without bumbling it.

Taking my letter down to the recreation room, I read through what I've already written — all this business about Ed wanting to adopt me and Aunt Millie saying no. I barely have time to begin my first new sentence before Nessa plunks herself down at the table beside me. She sounds out of breath, like maybe she's run all the way from the dormitory.

"I've got some things figured out," she says. Just as I form a loop around the "O" I'm writing, Nessa pulls the pencil from my fingers.

"Give me that!" I squawk, reaching to get it back.

"Not till you hear me out." Can't imagine that anything Nessa has to say is more important than me writing a letter to Evelyn. Leaning back in my chair, I cross my arms in front of me. Nessa looks from side to side and behind her. You'd think she was about to divulge top-secret information.

"Fine. What have you got figured out?" I snap, thinking this had better be good.

Leaning in close so that she's scarcely a nose length away, she whispers, "I think Miss Turner could be your mother."

Chapter Thirteen

Evidence to prove that Beth Turner, alias Brenda Turple, is Cammie Turple's mother, as put forth by Vanessa Matilda Maxwell:

1. *Miss Turner has blonde hair as does Cammie Turple.*
2. *Miss Turner wears glasses — eye problems are inherited.*
3. *Miss Turner has blue eyes like Cammie Turple.*
3. ~~*Cammie Turple and Miss Turner are both sleepwalkers.*~~
4. *Miss Turner's initials are BT — the same as Brenda Turple's. (She probably changed her name to throw people off her trail.)*
5. *Miss Turner got all flustered when Cammie mentioned Aunt Millie. It's obvious they know each other. Why would she lie about that? And how could they possibly know each other?*
6. *Miss Turner lives on Burnham Street — the same as Cammie's mother. Coincidence? I think <u>not</u>.*

I rest my case. Let the evidence speak for itself.

Ever since we found out Miss Turner lives on Burnham, Nessa's been convinced that she's my mother. I thought she was joking until she presented me with a list of evidence.

"Hey, I was only pretending to sleepwalk!" I yelp, crossing number four off the list. Nessa shrugs. Since I'm not about to believe Miss Turner could do something so cruel as to dump me out at Aunt Millie's, I agree to come to Nessa's house for the weekend to put an end to any further speculation on her part.

"Ouija will settle this for us once and for all," she says at the tail end of her invitation.

"And if it says Miss Turner's not really Brenda, you'll back off?"

"You won't hear another peep from me," says Nessa, sounding a little too confident for my liking.

If it takes some stupid board to convince Nessa that there's no way Miss Turner could be my long-lost pop-me-out-and-leave-me mother, then so be it. Let the truth be known.

―

Life has a way of dragging you through a knothole backwards. I didn't know what those words meant the first time Herb Winters said them. But what I didn't know back then I'm making up for now. I've surely gone through that knothole a time or two since arriving here at the school. This week seems to be one of those times.

I figure something's in the works when I get word that Mr. Allen wants to talk to me. It's been days since our muddled attempt at calling a cab, so I'm pretty sure it has nothing to do with that. I've been making my bed every morning, so that can't be it either. I even comb Jennie and Rebecca's hair in the morning and button their blouses just to help the maids out. (Turns out Jennie's naturally curly hair isn't nearly as natural as I imagined. Still, it doesn't stop me from admiring it up close. Curly beats out limp and straight any time of day.)

My brain picks through all the things that have happened this last while, looking for something I've done that would land me in trouble. Coming up empty-handed doesn't stop the queasiness I've got as I walk through the doorway of Mr. Allen's office.

Mr. Allen smiles and tells me to take a seat. He asks how I like it here and if I'm making lots of friends. I take a breath — so far so good. This chitchat is just to throw me off. He's working up to his real business, treading into it nice and easy the way grown-ups sometimes do. His words come out like a conversation about the weather — smooth and relaxed, catching me off guard. I could come up with a number of scenarios but never would I expect Mr. Allen to say that Ed's coming to see me this weekend.

"He'll be here Sunday afternoon. Now, isn't that nice?" Nice isn't exactly the word I'd use to describe what I'm feeling at the moment. Not that I won't be glad to see Ed — I'm just not sure how I feel about this whole adoption thing Aunt Millie's been going on about. I can't figure out why Ed would want to adopt me now. Why the sudden interest in making it legal? There has to be more to this than Aunt Millie is letting on — some other reason her drawers are twisted in a knot. But sometimes ignoring a problem is the only thing left to do when you run out of ideas on how to solve it. I'd already decided I'm not going to bring the subject of adoption up when next I see Ed. Besides, what if Ed hasn't booed a word about adoption? It certainly wouldn't be the first time Aunt Millie's stretched the truth.

"Thank you kindly for the offer, Mr. Allen," I say after he springs this business about Ed on me, "but I'm supposed to go home with Nessa this weekend. I even have permission."

If I can skin out of this meeting with Ed — at least postpone it for a little while — maybe I can settle this whole business about Miss Turner being my mother this weekend. Problems solve best when you handle them one at a time. Besides, who's to say Ed won't bring Miranda with him? I've been giving her some thought at night when I'm lying awake staring at the ceiling. Has Ed even mentioned me to her and the fact that I can't see so well? Could be she'll think I'm a burden, a leftover from the days when Ed was in love with another woman.

"I see," says Mr. Allen, his words stiff as a parlour poker. A few seconds pass before he lets me have it with a double shot of guilt right to the midsection.

"Don't you suppose you should put your visit with Vanessa off for another time since your father wants to come all the way into the city to see you? It must be important to him — don't you think?"

"Important? To Ed? Probably not." I give a shrill laugh, trying to lighten the mood. It wasn't the right thing to do. Mr. Allan's body language tells it all.

"I'm afraid you'll have to put your weekend off this time, Cammie," Mr. Allen says. "I've already told Mr. Hanover that he'd be most welcome to come. I can't have him driving all the way here for nothing. You should be happy to have your father come visit. Our parents do far more for us than most of us are aware of. It's part of the responsibility of having a child."

I want to speak up and say that Ed really hasn't had the chance to take much responsibility for me, but some things are best left unsaid. I really wanted to put this business about Miss Turner behind me. Now I'll have to wait. Too bad Nessa hadn't kept her ideas to herself. There are no cold hard facts to back this whole case up, just a lukewarm speculation on Nessa's part. I bet her father, being a lawyer, would have something to state about that. While a big part of me thinks it sounds far-fetched, I keep getting jabbed by a finger of a thought that says, regardless of how unlikely it all sounds, maybe, just maybe, it's true.

When I point out that Mrs. Maxwell has made plans for us to have a tea party and is already knee-deep in planning what squares to bake, Mr. Allen isn't the least bit perturbed.

"I'm sure Mrs. Maxwell isn't about to stand in the way of you visiting with your father. Don't you worry, she'll understand." He gives me a big old grin. He's not going to budge. Case closed. I've lost out again.

Chapter Fourteen

"Nervous?" Ed asks, looking over at me with a shining big grin on his face.

I stop twisting the ends of my hair. "Nah," I say, like it's no big deal to be driving around Halifax with Ed behind the wheel.

"I've never been much for city driving but I can get where I want to go," he says, looking over at me. I don't much care for the fact that he's paying more attention to me than his driving.

"Just keep your eyes on the road." I cringe for a tiny moment at the sound of my own voice, harsh the way Aunt Millie's is most of the time. But I don't want to start blubbering and ruin the whole day, so I've got to make myself sound tough as owl meat. Toughness keeps the tears from flowing. It's not like I'm going to get all choked up just because Ed's trying too hard.

Seeing Ed waiting in the lobby by the grandfather clock today kind of stopped me in my tracks. I didn't even know I was missing him until I was standing an arm's length away. He tousled my hair and asked who cut it, which kind of broke the ice. I was hoping he wouldn't give me a hug, but having him touch my head the way he did was nice. Ed seems to know the right thing to do. Then I yammered on about all the things we get to do here, like swimming and manual training class, piano lessons for anyone who's musically inclined. He finally suggested we go for a drive. It's not like me to rattle on like that. No wonder Ed shut me up.

"Did I ever tell you about the time I hitchhiked to Yarmouth on the back of a potato truck?" says Ed as we drive along. When I don't say anything he asks if I heard him.

"Of course I heard. I'm not deaf." I sit staring at the road ahead. The streets are filled with traffic — cars and trucks, all colours and sizes, everyone with a destination in mind. Then there's Ed and me just driving around on a Sunday afternoon with nowhere in particular to be.

I've got no right being snarky, but Ed can drag out a story like nobody else I know. On the chance this is going to be one of those stories, I try not to encourage him any. I've got more important thoughts in my head, like wondering when he's going to bring up this whole subject of adoption. Not to mention that, unlike everyone else on the road, he probably hasn't got a clue where he's going.

Ed turns the wheel and a car honks its horn. When he comes to a stop sign I'm pitched forward in my seat. When he steps on the gas, back I go. He keeps right on talking like there's nothing more important than the story he's telling.

"Do you know what I did when my stomach got to rumbling?" he asks. I shake my head. At least he got us this far without running into something.

"I just peeled myself a potato. Darn near ate though a fifty-pound bag before we got there. I'd have given a dollar for a sprinkle of salt. Can't say old Tom Jefferson appreciated it any." Ed lets out a queer laugh, like he's back there living it all over again.

A fifty-pound bag of potatoes — like I'd believe that! Okay, so I've got to laugh at Ed and his ridiculous story. Still jabbering away, he starts telling me things about when he was growing up, like I'm interested in something that happened a hundred years before I was born. He's stalling for time and we both know it.

"Want an ice cream?" he asks, finally parking the truck, like I'd ever in a million years refuse that.

Gulls screech overhead. I can make out some boats down in the harbour, so big they'd be impossible to miss. The air brings the goosebumps out on my arms even though I've got my warm coat on. I didn't know we were this close to the water. The sea air smells salty. We go into a little diner and step up to the counter. I puff up like a bullfrog when Ed says he wants a double-scoop ice cream for his best girl. We sit by the window looking out at the busy street, people walking by in a hurry. Strange how living at the school can make you forget you're in a city full of people. Being in a place where everyone understands you, and everything is all planned out, makes you feel so safe.

Ed asks a million questions and then some, like how my grades are and what my best subject is. We laugh about silly things and he tells me some more of his stories. I tell him about the boys sitting on the other side of the classroom and he laughs. Without missing a beat, I tell him that the boys learn piano tuning and chair caning. The best way to avoid certain subjects is to keep the conversation moving. He asks how the food is and what time I have to go to bed. Just when I start thinking that this whole nonsense about adoption is just that — nonsense — Ed starts to get serious on me. His voice drops and he rubs the back of his neck. He clears the phlegm out of his throat a few times and I kind of hope he doesn't spit.

I jump up from the table before he has time to drop any bombshells on me. "We should probably get back," I croak, as something squeezes my throat. Ed tells me to sit back down; he's got something to talk over with me.

"I've got a proposition for you," he says, like he's about to make a business deal.

"I know what you're going to say," I cut him off. "Aunt Millie already blabbed. I talked to her on the pay phone a few weeks back."

I can't say the word "adopt" out loud. It wouldn't make it past my tonsils. All those years thinking no one wanted me — I'm too scared to let myself hope.

"Should have known Millie wouldn't keep quiet," says Ed, shaking his head. I pay attention to his coal black hair instead of what he's saying. If I concentrate on something else maybe it will be okay. He touches my hand.

"I'm just asking you to think it over, Cammie. It would mean I'd be responsible for you. Millie wouldn't have the whole say in things — she wouldn't have any say. That might not be such a bad thing." Ed clears his throat. "It wouldn't be just you and me, though. I met someone a while back...Her name's Miranda. You'll really like her." There's a spark in Ed's voice I've never heard before. I haven't got the heart to tell him Aunt Millie blabbed all that too. No one wants someone raining on their parade.

"Would I have to live with you?" I'm not looking to leave the school, not after the rigmarole I went through to get here. Then, too, there's Miranda to consider. Maybe she isn't as gung-ho about this as Ed is. Not to mention I'm settling in and have lots of friends at the school. This business of weighing out the pros and cons of Ed's idea is of the utmost seriousness.

"Only during the summer months. I think it would be best if you stayed here at the school the rest of the year — you would come home for Christmas, of course." I squirm in my seat. "That's if you want to. Really, it's up to you, Cammie. You're the one who'll be affected the most."

My head is a wrinkled mess of thoughts and I try to iron them out. When something sounds too good to be true it usually is.

"What about Aunt Millie?"

"She'll have to get used to it — if you say yes, that is. She's not your mother...but I'm your father. That should count for more in any court of law."

"But how? I mean, what would we do?" If I get my hopes up and this thing falls apart I'll die for sure. Aunt Millie can put the binders on anything when she sets her mind to it. She's already told Ed no.

"I could apply to the court," says Ed. He stops and I know there's something more coming. "There's just one thing — I need your birth record and Millie won't give it up."

Big surprise. Did Ed really expect Aunt Millie to cooperate?

"I'm at a dead end for the time being, at least," says Ed, rubbing the back of his neck. "Miranda wrote to the Registrar General but they have no record — nothing to show a baby was born to Brenda Turple on December 3rd, 1939. Millie says she doesn't have it but I don't believe her. There has to be a record somewhere. And look at me: this isn't your problem to solve. I'll figure something out, I promise."

A blast of hope bursts inside me. "Aunt Millie has a wooden box in her room...The rhinestone necklace Drew bought her. I used to take it out when she wasn't around. There was a paper. I remember it. At the bottom. But I couldn't read it." My tongue is going at a hefty rate as it tries to keep pace with my brain. I might not even be making sense.

"That *could* be it." Ed sound cautious.

"Aunt Millie never keeps papers. It would have to be important. I can look...at Christmas when I go home." If I'm the one who has to get this show on the road then so be it. I look up at Ed. He's smiling.

"Do you think Miranda will like me?" I ask.

"What's not to like?" he says, and I think maybe I'll explode with joy right on the spot.

Chapter Fifteen

I whisper that the coast is clear. In one slick movement, Nessa opens the hall closet. "Hurry!" I say, waving her on while craning my neck to make sure the hallway is still empty. From the kitchen comes a string of tiny pops, and the smell of fresh-popped corn wafts up the hallway. My mouth waters. I haven't had popcorn since last Christmas, when Aunt Millie got it into her head to make some way late at night. When the smoke started rolling from the pot, I grabbed it out of her hands.

Aunt Millie makes popcorn the same way she looks after me: without paying too much attention. She squawked and gave me a slap on the arm, snatching the pot away like she was grabbing up precious stones. She insisted on adding the melted butter even though the popcorn was ruined — burnt black as the bottom of a kettle by the smell of it.

"Ruined, schmuined," she snapped. "It'll be just fine." When I refused to try any she made a wild dive for the bowl, and the popcorn went flying through the air.

"Now look what you made me do!" she cried. Storming out of the kitchen, she left me to clean up the mess. The smell of scorched popcorn was still in the kitchen the next morning.

"Come on," I urge as Nessa reaches up on the closet shelf. It won't be long and the corn will all be popped. Mrs. Maxwell could show up at any moment.

"Got it!" says Nessa, pulling it down. We scurry for her bedroom like field mice. I can tell she's done this a time or two.

To say I was relieved when Nessa sent her mother down to the kitchen to make popcorn would be an understatement. I'm not used to having someone hovering around asking questions. But you can hardly tell someone to get lost when they're in their own house, especially when you've only just made their acquaintance.

Ever since I arrived, Mrs. Maxwell has been hanging to us like barn scrapings to a shovel, asking me every question under the sun: where I'm from and do I have any brothers or sisters; whether I like it at the school; do I eat everything that's put in front of me; and how long have I been going to the school — since Nessa has never once mentioned my name. If I didn't know better, I'd have thought she was interviewing me for the newspaper.

At least Mr. Maxwell's working, even though it's Saturday evening. No worries about him putting in an appearance. Nessa says crooks don't take time off for weekends and neither does her father. To hear her talk he's the one out rounding up the bad guys, not helping to get them off scot-free.

Never in a million years did I think I'd be asking dead people for their help. When Evelyn used to tell me about his brother, the shivers would start walking up my spine. Being in the same room as someone who's vapour and spirit is enough to put me on edge. Only Nessa says there's nothing to it.

"It's like having a conversation with an old friend."

I'll believe that when I see it — or don't see it.

"Dead people have a right to communicate too," she added. I ended up agreeing, like our conversation was making sense.

"You stay here and guard the board while I go for the popcorn," says Nessa, leaving me all alone. I don't bother to ask who she thinks I'm guarding it from. Taking advantage of her absence, I remove the top of the cardboard box and take a look inside. I shake my head the way Ed sometimes does. Hard to believe something that small can hold the answer to all the questions in the world. There are two words at the top. *Yes* on the left and *No* on the right. In the middle of the board are the letters of the alphabet. There's a star and a moon on the board. A heart-shaped object with three little legs is in the box. I pick it up for closer look, but decide it's best not to go poking around things that don't belong to me. Besides, I don't want to upset some ghost by playing around with things I know nothing about. Putting the lid back on, I wait for Nessa to bring on the popcorn. What can be taking so long?

I get off the bed and mosey around. The walls in Nessa's bedroom are enough to make most people gasp.

"Periwinkle," said Nessa earlier, like she could read my thoughts.

"Not bad," I said, trying not to sound too impressed.

I can hear Nessa in the kitchen talking to her mother, but can't make out what they're saying. The Maxwells have a fancy enough home, with lots of furniture and lacy white curtains, and blinds to keep the neighbours from looking in. There's a piano in the parlour and Nessa with a whole shelf full of dolls she doesn't seem to care about. Her father likely gets paid a bundle for getting thieves and murderers off the hook.

"Mother keeps on buying me dolls, but I'm too old," Nessa said when we first settled into her room. I caught myself ready to start gushing over them.

"Dolls are for kids," I agreed, reeling in my enthusiasm, pretending not to notice the pretty getups they were wearing. It must be nice to have so many dolls you don't give a care, though. I'd have settled for just one growing up.

Finally Nessa shows up toting a big bowl of popped corn. Shoving my hand in, I grab up some of the greasy goodness. My teeth squeak against a popped kernel as I chomp away. Just the right amount of butter and a smidge of salt; delicious. Mrs. Maxwell sure has Aunt Millie beat in the corn-popping department. I shove more into my mouth while waiting for instructions on summoning up spirits. Talking to ghosts is serious business. I have to stay on my toes. If there are any ghosts hanging around this board, they'd best be prepared to speak. Cammie Turple isn't about to be duped by some spirit she's never once met.

Chapter Sixteen

"Can you get it, Cammie girl?" Herb Winters would say. He'd stretch his palm out flat, and I always knew there'd be a shiny coin in the middle. I'd make a wild grab for it but he'd be too fast. He'd open his hand, tempting me to try again, and I would every time. We'd laugh, and at the end of it all he'd give me the coin. But having the coin was never the best part of our game.

Herb was kind of happy-go-lucky, always laughing and joking about something. He'd tell silly jokes that he'd heard at the Texaco station over in Sheppard Square, ones about wives and husbands, and people knocking at your door in the middle of the night. I never understood his jokes, but I'd laugh along with him. He'd sit at the table and drink moonshine until Aunt Millie would tell him it was time to go home. She usually didn't allow people into the house during the week, but for Herb she'd always make an exception.

The night Herb died, he'd sat at the kitchen table with Aunt Millie. They talked about sensible things, like the roadwork going on in Tanner and Aunt Millie thinking she might just get a telephone one of these days. Their discussion turned serious as the evening wore on, like is there life after death and just who would ever make it into heaven if there were?

I liked the way Aunt Millie sounded like a regular everyday person those times, a person who was someone's aunt, or neighbour, maybe even someone who knit socks on winter evenings or visited people who were sick. I got the idea that Herb knew more about her than the rest of us did, or else saw something in her we couldn't. Kind of like he knew the worst about her, all the prickles she showed the rest of the world, but he didn't care about any of that. I used to feel that I was the only one who'd take Aunt Millie the way she was until the night I heard them talking in the kitchen.

All night long Herb teetered back and forth on the chair. His eyes were little more than two slits he could barely keep open. If someone had come along and brushed him with a feather he'd have fallen over. When he saw me smiling at him he gave a wink.

"What's so funny, Cammie girl?" he asked, grinning.

The next morning, Aunt Millie came into my room and shook me awake.

"Herb's gone," she said, standing over me with her arms folded in front of her.

"Gone?" I wasn't sure what she meant.

"Gone. Dead. Drowned in a ditch, the poor fool. Didn't have the sense to get himself out."

I burst into tears.

"Don't bother grieving over Herb, Cammie. His was just a wasted life anyway," Aunt Millie said. Her voice had a queer sound to it, one I haven't heard since. She sat on the edge of my bed and laid her hand on my back for a long while. I'd never known someone who died before. I guess Aunt Millie figured it was a pretty big deal to me.

—

"The dead see everything and know everything, but some spirits are tricksters and like to play games. They'll make up things even if it's not the truth, so you have to be careful not to let these scoundrels in," says Nessa, giving me a quick rundown on what all ghosts can do if the mood hits them, like any of what she's saying sounds at all fair to me. There should be a few rules you have to follow once you're dead. Bad enough that dead people know everything about the living; why make up gossip while they're at it?

"Do you know someone who's dead? It works best if you can talk to someone you actually know." Nessa removes the board from the box, while chomping on a handful of popcorn. I think of Evelyn's older brother, Beecher, but shoot that idea down. I don't actually know him. Could be he'd think I was taking advantage of my friendship with Evelyn, seeing how he and I have never been properly introduced. Waiting to get acquainted with someone after they're dead wouldn't make for the best of circumstances — not to mention them knowing you were only talking to them in the first place because you want their help.

Just then I think of someone. "Herb Winters!" I say. We got along pretty good in the past, and other than Evelyn's brother, he's the only dead person I've had the opportunity to know.

"Now, you can't just talk to any old ghost that's around. It's got to be someone you'd trust to tell the truth," says Nessa as she continues to lay out all the rules.

"Hey, Herb was my friend!" How many dead people does she think I know? The pickings are mighty slim in that department. Besides, Herb can be trusted to tell the truth. That's the important thing.

Once Nessa shows me how to place my fingers on the heart-shaped pointer, we're ready to start.

"We have to keep our fingers on it at all times, but go lightly…very lightly, like when you're reading Braille," she says, without cracking a smile. I've never heard her sound so serious — and I've never read Braille before. Neither has Nessa for that matter. I bite the side of my lip to keep from laughing.

Nessa warms the board up by asking questions everyone would know the answer to, even someone who's been dead a few years. Apparently, like starting an old car, you can't expect it to take off without grinding a few gears. You've got to let it idle a little. I still have my doubts about this. It seems pretty silly to me.

"Now, you've got to be polite and call the spirit by name." I have to make myself be serious if this has even a chance of succeeding. While talking to ghosts has a lot of rules, I figure, silly or not, it'll be worth it to get Nessa off my case.

Eventually, Nessa works her way up to the matter at hand. "Ouija — are there any spirits out there?" she asks, looking out into space.

I wait for something to happen. I don't know what. The only experience I've had with spirits are the kind that comes in the bottles Aunt Millie used to have at the house, and thinking this makes me want to laugh all over again.

"I said, 'Ouija — are there any spirits out there?'" Nothing. No surprises, since I don't half believe any of this anyway. Nessa repeats her question. Again, nothing. A giggle pushes against the inside of my mouth and rubs against my ribs. I might not be able to hold it in. Just when I'm about to tell Nessa we should forget it, something quivers beneath my fingertips. Small but real, very real. I suck in my breath as the pointer all but floats across the board and stops on *Yes*. I yank my fingers off the board and shake them out. Nessa gives me a stern look, and I make contact with the pointer again. I straighten my shoulders. It's time to stop acting like a kid. My future is depending upon this. If I want to get my life straightened out, I have to snap to attention.

"Ouija — do you know the girl sitting beside me?"

Another *Yes*.

"Can you spell out her name?"

Fright ploughs through me when the pointer moves to the "C" and doesn't stop until it has spelled out my entire name. This thing really does work! I can't hide now. Some ghost out there knows who I am. Hard to say what else it knows about me. I hold in another giggle. When you're starting down a scary path, sometimes the only thing that comes out of you is a laugh.

We make our introductions, and Nessa tells me to ask Ouija if Herb Winters is here. "He won't come if you don't ask him to," she says. Makes sense; Herb was never the pushy kind. Sometimes when there was a gang sitting around the kitchen he'd hardly open his mouth. He was more of a listener than a talker. Poor old Herb, I could miss him if I thought about him too hard.

"Ouija, is Mr. Herb Winters here?" The quiver in my throat makes me feel stupid. I wait for the pointer to start moving like it did when Nessa was asking the questions. It doesn't budge, not even a speck. I sigh and give it another go. Maybe it doesn't like me.

"Mr. Herb Winters," I repeat. Mister — Pfffff. How ridiculous, calling Herb mister. If he was here sitting beside me he'd be laughing like a fool. Nessa said to be all polite, but she didn't know Herb.

"Hey, Herb, how's it going? Are you anywhere near handy? I've got a favour to ask," I say real loud, remembering that he was sometimes hard of hearing.

"That's no way to talk to a spirit," says Nessa, puckering up her face.

"Well, it's the way I always talked to Herb." I give her back a look that could stop a bear in its tracks. I don't need Nessa telling me how to talk to old Herb.

Nessa's sigh isn't anywhere near loud enough to drown out my next, "Are you there, Herb Winters?" She might know how to talk to your run-of-the-mill spirits, but not Herb. Sometimes you've got to do things your own way no matter what the experts might tell you.

"Did you feel that?" I ask as the pointer wobbles. That

little nudge gives me confidence. I'll put on the Turple charm, roll him in slow and steady the same way Evelyn used to reel in a big whopper of a fish down at the river.

"I need your help, Herb. Are you there?" That nibble has me yearning for the next big bite. We wait. Patience is required when you're on a fishing expedition. I learned that much from Evelyn Merry. Hardly a fishing trip went by that he didn't catch something.

And then, like sliding on an icy pond, the pointer moves across the board to the upper corner and stops on *Yes*. I wiggle back and forth on the bed. Finally, we're getting somewhere. I have to hope Nessa knows what she's talking about, that a ghost knows all and tells all if you catch them in a good mood. Herb was always in a good mood whenever I saw him. I can't imagine all that has changed now that he's dead. I clear my throat. I have things to tell Herb Winters.

"I'm not living with Aunt Millie these days, Herb," I start in. I skim over most of the details — just hitting the high spots like when you're taking a bath. Sometimes the less you tell the less complicated things become. "I'm in the city at the blind school. Did you know that, Herb?" The pointer moves all around the board then rests again on the *Yes*. That brings a smile to my face. At least someone back home cares what I'm doing, even if that someone is dead.

"Ask him, ask him," says Nessa, like I'm going to let this moment of truth go without finding out what I want to know. Squirming a little, I get down to the matter at hand. A lot is riding on this one question, a whole lifetime's worth of spite — not to mention all the unanswered questions that have been festering in me for ages.

"I've been trying to locate my mother, Herb. She's somewhere in the city and I want to find her. Can you help?" This time the pointer shimmies. It moves around the board and stops on *Yes* again. By now I'm getting mighty excited. I'm almost too scared to think straight.

"There's a supervisor here at the school, Herb. Her name is Miss Turner. Nessa and I have been talking and, well, Nessa thinks she might be my mother. Is she my mother, Herb? Is Miss Turner really Brenda Turple?"

Nothing happens for a time. Maybe Herb's thinking it over, trying to decide if this information is something he dares to tell. The suspense is killing me. And then the pointer goes crazy, from one side of the board to the other and back again. It stops like someone suddenly ordered it to. My heart makes a double flip.

"I knew it!" squeals Nessa jumping up from the bed. "I just knew it!"

Chapter Seventeen

I know about the baby you gave away. Meet me at the Public Gardens at 3:00 this Saturday to discuss this and other matters — or else.

Writing with all the force I can muster, I cross my t's and dot my i's with eleven years of Turple spite urging me on. If the pencil I'm using snaps in two, I won't be surprised. There's plenty more in me to say, but I'm planning to save that for when we're standing face to face. Imagine finding out someone you thought was so nice is really a wolf living in sheep's wool. It pains me in a way I can't begin to describe. How could someone as sweet as Miss Turner have given her baby to Aunt Millie without guilt biting a big chunk out of her?

My tongue runs along the edge of the envelope. Currents of sheer nastiness tingle in my fingertips as I press it shut. On the envelope I write: *For Miss Turner's eyes only.*

Miss Turner! I let out a pfffff. She sure has everyone here fooled. Well, it's high time everyone finds out who she really is. I'm prepared to blow her lie right out of the water. This Saturday afternoon will be as good a time as any. She isn't any better than Aunt Millie when it comes right down to it — maybe worse. At least Aunt Millie isn't hiding her real self under a bunch of sugary words and syrupy smiles. At least with Aunt Millie what you see is what you get. Imagine pretending to be someone you aren't, changing your name and never looking back at your past. Worse than that is having her ignore me these weeks since she found out that her sister and my aunt Millie are one in the same. My very own mother, right under the same roof as me, and she didn't even bat an eyelash. I bet she never thought the secret she's been toting around all this time would land right here in her lap. I'll make her sorry she dumped me out at Aunt Millie's if it's the last thing I do.

Seeing how it's Miss Turner's day off, I make my way to the supervisor's sitting room with the envelope stuffed inside my navy blue tunic. I'm not about to get questioned about the letter I'm carrying. I've got more wits about me than that. The envelope crinkles near my chest as I walk along. Pulling this off will be a piece of cake with all the practice I've had sneaking out of Aunt Millie's house through the years. Nessa offered to come with me to deliver the letter, but this is a family matter, private business between mother and daughter, something I need to take care of all on my own.

The sitting-room door is closed. Opening it quickly, I step inside like a thief on the prowl. The room has a sweet aroma that reminds me of Evelyn Merry. The first time I came down for mail call I noticed the room smelled of honeysuckle. A big vine of it grows next to the Merrys' front verandah. Evelyn brought a handful of blossoms to our secret camp one day.

"I'm not much for smelling flowers," I told him. He chucked them outside before I had time to even sniff them properly, dusted his hands off like he'd been holding something dirty. Sometimes I wish I could get those moments back — too late once you've ruined them the first time around. There's never any going back to what was, or what could have been, because by the time you catch up to what you should have done it's already too late.

As light-footed as a water skip on a pond, I bound my way to the desk and place the envelope where it's sure to be seen. Seeing how there isn't much for clutter on the desk, that shouldn't present a problem. Looking down at the envelope, a hiccough of joy bubbles inside me. *Just you wait, Brenda Turple*, I think to myself. *Just you wait.*

Being hot on my mother's trail, it's hard to focus on anything else. My mind wanders away during morning assembly. While Nessa plays her piano piece, I can't even hear if she's making any mistakes. Me, I'm in the Public Gardens telling Brenda about my crummy childhood living in a bootlegger's house. Later, while Mr. Allen reads another chapter from *Beautiful Joe*, I'm laughing in Brenda's face, telling her about Ed's plan to adopt me. Funny all the things you can do without having to leave your chair.

When I make silly mistakes in mathematics class, Mrs. Craig asks me if my mind's been on holiday this week. Spelling class isn't much better. When you're tracking a person's movements, it's hard to think of anything else.

On Thursday evening, who should come moseying on into the recreation room without a care in the world but Miss Turner. Two days until the big showdown, you can bet she's squirming like a worm on a hook — and me the fish about to grab her. She comes over and it takes a mountain of willpower to keep from saying something snotty right there in front of everyone. But I'm waiting for the right time and that right time is Saturday afternoon. Instead, I say, "Hi, Miss Turner," like the rest of the girls. I don't want to blow my cover.

Jennie has her autograph book out and you just can't help laughing at some of the verses written there. *When you get old and cannot see, I'll hold the pot so you can pee* puts us all in stitches for a time.

Jennie says she wants me to write something in her book, but I tell her I don't know any verses. "Besides, I want to find one you don't already have," I say, which seems to please her as much as when we're served bread pudding for dessert. An autograph is a big responsibility and takes some serious thought. Once something's written down there's no taking it back. It's there for a lifetime and I like to think I'll be remembered for more than holding someone's pot for them to pee in, no matter how funny it might sound. Not to mention I'm not at all acquainted with autograph books or the verses that go into them, seeing how the girls back in Tanner never gave me the time of day.

"Here's one you could write, Cammie," says Miss Turner, butting in like I'd be interested in her help. "Old friends are like diamonds, precious and rare; false friends are like autumn leaves, strewn everywhere." I tell her no offense but I'm planning to ask my aunt Millie for her help. I'm not surprised that she doesn't hang around long after that.

Nessa keeps asking me what I'm going to say to Miss Turner, because facing your enemy doesn't happen just any old day of the week.

"I haven't yet decided," I say, flexing the upper hand I now have. And really, how can you plan out what to say when you're not sure what kinds of lame excuses you'll be given in return?

That little bird inside me has been fluttering like crazy ever since Herb told me the truth about my mother. Coming from someone else I might have questioned it, but when he was alive, Herb never gave me reason to question anything he said. I doubt he'd make up anything now that he's dead. Besides, there'd be no reason for him to lie to me now. It's not like a dead person would have anything to gain.

Friday night comes and I can't stop myself from flouncing around in bed. Tomorrow's the big day, the showdown I've pictured in my mind for the longest while. I can't stop talking to Miss Turner in my head. Each conversation we have is a little different, usually with me telling her what a horrible mother's she's been. I try to state things just right, figure out which words will cause her the most pain. Sometimes I jump right into the middle of a conversation where she's begging me to forgive her and me, I just laugh in her face. I walk away. She calls me back, pleading for me not to tell her secret. When your world is closing in around you, there's every reason for you to squirm.

Chapter Eighteen

The sun cracks through the November clouds as Nessa and I walk to the Public Gardens. Seems like a good sign, like maybe God's smiling down at me. I'm about to be finished with my old life for good. All those loose threads will be tied up good and tight. I'll be moving on once and for all, wiping my hands clean of this whole mess called my past.

"I'll take you to the Public Gardens but I won't listen in," said Nessa when we made our plans for the day. Not that I figured she'd be nosy enough to involve herself in my affairs, but not everyone would understand. It's hard to speak your mind with someone listening in.

The trees are hanging with colour — red, yellow, and orange. We walk through a cemetery: a shortcut, according to Nessa. Although I'd rather not have to pass all these spooky grey tombstones, I keep my uncertainties to myself. If Nessa doesn't mind, neither do I.

Looking up into the sky, I smile back big and wide in a thanks-for-everything kind of way. When you're about to get the very thing you've wanted for as long as you can remember, you can't help but feel on top of the world. The envelope with Brenda's address on it crinkles as I walk. I shove my hand in my pocket. My proof. It's the only link I have to my mother, the one thing she messed up that ended up leading me straight to her. I want to rub it in her face and ask her how it feels to have her past finally catch up with her.

Nessa's house is within walking distance of the park. City slickers like Nessa talk about going to the park like it's something special, but back in Tanner the whole outdoors is one big old park.

"I'd go with you girls if this wasn't Mrs. Howard's day to stop by," said Mrs. Maxwell. I sent a sly look Nessa's way. The last thing we wanted was her mother stepping in on my business. Nessa timed our rendezvous with Miss Turner right down to a T. Mrs. Howard never misses a Saturday afternoon visit at the Maxwells'. She's as regular as Old Faithful, that geyser up north Mrs. Larkin told us about last week in geography. Having Mrs. Maxwell with us would have put a damper on our whole scheme. Battling your enemy is serious dealings for anyone, and you don't want any witnesses keeping track of the causalities.

We hurry along lickety-split, arms locked, in a one-for-all-and-all-for-one kind of way. What could be a nail-biting situation, one that should have me as skittish as a cat, just has me raring to get it over with. I'm about to face the person who ditched me right after I was born, let her know just how crummy I think she is, and free up all the feelings I've been carrying with me. My heart should be hammering up a storm. But me, I'm looking forward to it.

Miss Turner wasn't at the school on Friday. Mrs. Skinner said she'd come down with a bug. A bug, all right — a bug called Cammie Turple. It doesn't take a genius to figure out the pressure finally got to her.

"Maybe she'll be too sick to come to the park," says Nessa.

"Oh, she'll be there — a Turple never backs away from a fight," I say, cracking my knuckles. "I've got her right where I want her."

By the time we reach the park I'm wondering just how I'll start things off. When you're ready to pounce, all those nerves and muscles are just itching to let go. Nessa says not to worry because when you're on the side of good, the right words find you. I have to assume she knows what she's talking about.

"Is she here?" I ask, craning my neck. There are muddled shapes in the distance. I'm not so sure what they are, this being my first time to the Public Gardens. I can make out someone standing beside a bright red bush, but I can't tell if it's a man or a woman, let alone if it's Miss Turner.

"It's only a little past two thirty — you said three. Where did you tell her to meet you?"

Meet me? I smack my forehead with the palm of my hand. Why didn't I think of that when I was writing the note?

"I just said the Public Gardens. 'Meet me at the Public Gardens at three.'" Great! I've messed it up big time. If I could kick my own rear end I would. The park is a pretty big place. My mother would have to be a mind reader for this to work out right. I wring my hands. A single word from Nessa about how stupid I am could start me bawling like a baby. I chew at the side of my cheek, trying to stuff the disappointment back in.

"You're getting worked up over nothing. She's probably not here yet. We left early, remember?"

"But what if she's already here? What if we've missed her? She could be roaming around the park by now and we'll never find her." My luck, she's one of those people who shows up with hours to spare, twiddling her thumbs just waiting for the action to get underway. But then I take a deep breath and quickly come up with a plan. I've come too far to let a little setback shake me up.

"We'll hang out at the park entrance. When she comes through we'll see her. It'll be fine," I say, gathering up some confidence.

We stroll around in a casual style. I've never seen so many strange colours in all my life. Makes me wonder what they've got for trees here in the city, a lot different from what we've got back in Tanner. I almost gasp at a pink bush rounded up like an umbrella, but I don't want to sound childish in front of Nessa.

Seeing what time of year it is, visitors to the park are as scarce as hen's teeth. When someone walks through, I jump.

"Calm down, Cammie, it's just someone walking their dog," says Nessa. After a spell we sit down on a bench, me trying to play it nice and cool.

"Do you think she'll come?" Time's a-wasting and still no sign of her. Maybe she isn't as feisty as Aunt Millie. Or maybe Nessa's right, and she really *is* sick. Just as I'm thinking she's not going to put in an appearance, Nessa elbows me in the ribs; not enough to make me howl, but enough to make me sit up and take notice.

"There she is — I'm sure of it. That's her blue coat. I'd recognize it anywhere," says Nessa. I jump to my feet and suck in a big breath of air.

"Here goes nothing," I say, hurrying straight toward the blue jacket. I'm stopped in my tracks by a "Cammie" up ahead of me that sounds more like a question than a statement. It *is* Miss Turner. Nessa was right!

"What are you doing here? Do you have permission to be off school property?"

"I'm staying at Nessa's this weekend," I state, snappy-like — she has no reason to be concerned about my welfare this late in the game. If she'd been at school yesterday she'd probably know all that. She looks out past me then down at her wristwatch, jumpy as a cat on a midnight prowl. Me, I'm playing it calm. I'm on the side of good, and good always wins over evil. I have nothing to fear.

"You'll have to excuse me, Cammie, but I'm supposed to meet someone. I really can't stay and talk." She looks over her shoulder like she's afraid she's being watched. Too bad for her, but she's looking her enemy in the face and doesn't even know it.

Let the squirming begin.

"Oh, I think you'll want to talk to me." It's time to state my purpose, let her have it with both barrels. "Bet you never dreamed in a million years I'd be smart enough to figure it all out."

"Figure what out?"

I want to laugh.

"Surprised that I'm in on your deepest, darkest secret, the one you don't want anyone to know about?" Standing on my toes, I shove my face up close to hers. She pulls back like she's stepped on a hot potato in her bare feet.

"I don't know what you mean, Cammie. I don't have any secrets from you." The trembling in her voice is music to my ears, and I move in for the kill. A big old smile is bearing down on me but I hold it in. You can't look tough with your lips stretched out.

"Look here, Brenda," I say, using Aunt Millie's rock-candy voice, how I think she'd sound right about now if she were in my shoes. My finger is wagging in the air. Desperate times call for desperate measures, as Evelyn Merry likes to say.

"Brenda? I'm Beth — not Brenda. And you shouldn't be using my first name."

Her confusion sounds almost genuine. She's trying to throw me off. I could feel a little sorry for her if I didn't know the truth, how she went on with her life and forgot all about me.

"You mean Beth, otherwise known as Brenda, don't you? I know who you are. You can't fool me." She clams up tight for a few minutes and looks down at me like she's trying to come up with the perfect lie.

"Cammie, I don't know what you're talking about, but I've got to go." She starts to take off on me. I have to do something or she'll be gone and nothing will be settled. She isn't going to slip away from me like she did the first time around.

"You aren't going anywhere. I need you to hear what I've got to say." My words bunch up on me, coming out in quick bursts.

"I don't have time for this, Cammie. It's nearly three," she says, hurrying away from me. I take off after her, grabbing fast to her hand to make her stop, but she shakes me off.

My brain kicks into gear and I call out real fast before she gets away from me for the second time in my life: "You had a baby twelve years ago and you just walked away." That does it. Reeling around in the path, she's finally ready to listen to what I have to say.

"That's just plain ridiculous. There's no possible way you could know what you're talking about." Her voice is high-pitched like the squealing of a pig come butchering day.

"Oh yeah? Well, I know all about the baby you had," I say, closing the gap between us. Tears run down my cheeks, and I swat them away. No way am I going to let this get to me. The truth is on my side. And it's going to set me free.

"Why are you doing this, Cammie?"

"Someone's got to."

"People make mistakes in life. We all do." Her voice is quivering like jelly on a plate, but I don't let that influence me.

"Well now *your* mistake is looking *you* in the face."

"Cammie, dear, you're not making any sense."

"Don't 'Cammie dear' me. Are you denying you had a baby that you threw away?"

"Threw away?" Her words come out like sparks from a campfire. Pulling a hanky from her pocket, she lifts her glasses and dabs at her eyes, sniffing like she suddenly has a cold. I want to keep throwing words at her, get every last thing I've been thinking off my chest. I've seen people cry before. A few tears don't fizz me none.

"That's what I said. Threw away. Dumped out. It doesn't change what you did."

"And I've regretted it ever since — but how did you find out? No one knows…" She swallows a giant gulp of air. Her words trail away like dandelion fluff in the breeze, and she scrunches her face up at me. "Millie!" She gasps like the sudden pop of an overblown balloon. "But she said she'd never tell."

Chapter Nineteen

A sigh escapes Miss Turner's lips, as uneven as the pot holder I cut out in manual training class a few weeks back. Good. The sound of that sigh is music to my ears. I'm ready to fly at her like that old bantam rooster Evelyn's father use to have — so touchy it would come after you the moment you walked past.

"Confession is good for the soul," I cry out, something the minister said last week in church, even though I'm not completely sure what it means.

"Okay, you're right, Cammie," she says, throwing her arms up in the air. "Is that what you want me to say?" Her sudden admission shoots through me like an arrow. "I had a baby at a home for unwed mothers. That's where I met your aunt Millie. But I didn't throw my baby away. He was adopted out. I've regretted it ever since. There — are you happy now?"

The breeze comes to a screeching halt. Something catches up deep in the centre of me like a hiccough that won't let go.

"You had a *boy*?" I squeak out. My theory crumbles apart like brown sugar in milk.

"Yes, Cammie, I had a boy and I miss him every day."

"But — but you live on Burnham Street. My mother lives on Burnham Street." I pull out the envelope and hand it to her.

"Where did you get this?" Miss Turner examines the envelope.

"It came in the mail one day when I was small. Aunt Millie said it was from my mother. She burned the letter but I kept the envelope all these years."

Her blonde curls move as she shakes her head. "Oh, Cammie, I wrote that letter on a whim years ago. Millie said she was leaving Tanner but I took a chance. We were friends. I thought it would be nice to hear from her. When she didn't answer I thought for sure she'd moved away like she'd planned. So I didn't even put two and two together until you mentioned your aunt's name."

There's a queer feeling you get in the pit of your stomach when the pieces of your life come together too fast and you're trying to jam them into place before any of them get lost on you. But when you start to see that none of those pieces fit the way they're supposed to, that's the queerest feeling there is. All this time I thought my mother had written to find out how I was doing. Why would Aunt Millie lie like that? Things could start spinning out of control if I don't do something to stop it. Old Herb was wrong. Miss Turner isn't my mother at all. Funny how you can be so close to knowing a person's secret yet be a million miles off at the same time.

Dread curls ugly fingers around my heart and squeezes tight as I gather this information and put it in its proper place. Miss Turner had a boy. She met Aunt Millie at a home for unwed mothers. *She* wrote the letter, not my mother. The blood in my veins runs cold. This is the worst news imaginable — the very worst. My head spins and I can hardly think straight. When you're facing your most secret fear your mind doesn't work like it should.

A crow caws out from the treetops, and a handful of wind slaps me in the face. It doesn't take much brainpower to figure out the rest of the story. I don't want to hear what Miss Turner has to say about Aunt Millie and her reason for being at that home for unwed mothers.

"I've got to go…I've just got to go," I say.

When your world is caving in you don't stop to consider the consequences, you just do the first thing that comes into your head.

I race through the park without a thought as to where I'm going, past all the yellows, pinks, and oranges that I first thought were so pretty. My brain says *run, run, run* as my feet hit the dirt trail. From behind me, Nessa is shouting but I don't care. A hodgepodge of colours continues to whirl past me, melding into a single blur that I can't pick apart and make sense of. A tall grey figure up ahead draws me to it like a magnet. It might be a statue but I don't have time to find out. Darting past it, I have no plans to stop anytime soon. Not until I'm as far away from Miss Turner as I can get.

There's a large black patch on the path in front of me. Charging toward it, a fluttering sound fills the air. Hundreds of birds scatter in front of me, flapping their wings to find a safe place among the tree branches. All I can think about is going back home, finding Evelyn Merry, hashing this whole thing over with him. But I don't have Evelyn or his sensible way. He's not here to tell me that everything will be okay even when I'm sure there's no possible way it can be. I miss Evelyn Merry more than anything imaginable. He's the only one who knows the real Cammie Turple. Nessa's a good enough friend but she'll never take his place. Evelyn and me have been through too much together. Now, I have only myself to rely on and a whole bunch of new questions dogging me. If someone were to touch me I'd collapse on the spot.

My throat aches and my chest heaves each time my foot hits the ground. No wonder Aunt Millie didn't want Ed to adopt me. Ed — is he in on this too? Did he go along with Aunt Millie's story just to keep her quiet? But no, he wouldn't be talking about adopting me if he knew. Ed — what's he going to say about all this? Does this mean he's not my father after all? I cross the walking bridge over the pond. Nessa's yelling out at me but I just can't stop. When your life is dissolving around you there's not much else you care about.

I run so fast I don't think I'll ever stop. Strange sounds are coming out of me, sounds I don't even recognize. Aunt Millie's lies circle around me, poking fun each time my foot slaps the ground. Pieces of the past nip at my heels — nearly twelve years' worth of deceit and trickery — pushing me to run even harder. My old life flashes before me, things I never wanted to think about again. No matter what I do, or how hard I try, things are never going to change. I'll always be Cammie Turple from Tanner. Only now I'd give just about anything to be the bootlegger's niece, and that's something I never thought I'd ever end up saying.

My chest feels like someone reached in and pulled my ribs apart. Nessa gains on me, yelling for me to slow down. I'd like to stop, I really would, but my legs and heart won't let me. Miss Turner's voice mixes in with Nessa's as the truth starts closing in.

I push harder and harder as Nessa's voice drops farther behind me. I might just get away. But then my toe stubs up against something in my path and I'm sent flying. Seconds later, I crash down to earth. The burning in my palms and knees isn't nearly as bad as the one in my chest. From behind feet thump against the ground, stopping suddenly beside me.

"Are you okay?" asks Nessa, slowly helping me up off the ground. My head is spinning.

"I'm fine," I say, trying to loosen myself from her grip with my hands and knees still smarting.

"You could have been hurt, Cammie. Are you sure you're all right?" asks Miss Turner as she catches up to us. The tables have suddenly turned and now Miss Turner is holding all the cards. She should have scrammed when she had the chance. She's not my mother. That's all I need to know.

Fear, disappointment, and confusion are circling like a swarm of mosquitoes. Heaving and snuffing, I'm holding back the tears as best I can.

"Why did you run away from me?" asks Miss Turner.

"Because I don't want you to tell me."

"Don't want me to tell you what?" Miss Turner puts an arm around my shoulder. My legs go to mush. Pushing down a lump the size of a watermelon, I pull in a deep breath.

"I don't want you to tell me Aunt Millie's really my mother."

Chapter Twenty

"You've got this whole thing all wrong, Cammie. Millie *worked* at the home — she didn't go there to have a baby. She came in one day on the bus and was hired right on the spot. They were so short of staff. All those babies to look after in the nursery."

My mind slows to a crawl at this information. Miss Turner's words are like raindrops hitting a bit of sun-parched ground. I want to drink in her words because they taste so good. Thinking Aunt Millie might really be my mother felt like the end of the world. But imagining Aunt Millie having a regular, everyday job — well, that's enough to make even the sternest person giddy. Not to mention the relief I'm feeling at the moment now that I know she's not my mother. At least Aunt Millie didn't lie about that.

We find a bench where we won't be disturbed, right next to the pond. Colours reflect upon the water like a mirror.

I can't make out where the trees stop and the water starts. Ducks huddle in one corner, gossiping back and forth, sharing secrets like the old biddies down at Mae Cushion's store. Running away was a babyish thing to do. It's time for me to get tough, to hear the real truth about my life, no matter what that truth turns out to be. All this guessing and thinking and wondering is for the ducks. I'm ready to face the facts. With luck, Miss Turner will fill in some of the missing pieces of my life, the ones Aunt Millie protects like a mother bear. I can't pick and choose my past, or trade it in for something I like better. But maybe Miss Turner's version will help me make sense of the things Aunt Millie told me over the years, like how my mother left me back in Tanner and never once felt the need to check on me — not once. When you're getting down to the particulars there's a lot of digging and scraping to do before you reach the bottom.

"Did you know my mother?" I ask with crossed fingers.

Miss Turner shakes her head. "Millie asked everyone about her sister, but no one there remembered her. People came and went all the time from that place. And then they gave us new names when we arrived — to protect our privacy."

"But Aunt Millie knew *your* name. You wrote to her."

"We became friends, and friends confide in one another." Friends, Aunt Millie and Miss Turner? It seems so unlikely.

Aunt Millie never had any women friends that I knew of. She was always too busy selling moonshine.

There's nothing easy about this for either of us. My heart feels as tight as a fiddle string as I wait to hear the rest of the story. Miss Turner's hand reaches out for mine and she squeezes it gently. I can't imagine I ever believed she was my heartless mother.

She tells me about the home for unwed mothers where she met Aunt Millie, and how scary it was being away from home for the first time.

"The people who ran the place were nice enough, but it wasn't like being home. My parents paid my way, but they didn't visit or even write in case someone would discover my secret. I felt so alone until Millie came there to work. She really was a dear."

A dear? That doesn't sound like Aunt Millie to me. I could make a snotty comment, but I just let Miss Turner keep going. By keeping my mouth shut I'll find out where I fit into the picture. I'm sure of it. Then it will be my time to ask questions — not now.

Miss Turner clears her throat. "I didn't want to give my baby away, but my parents insisted." Her voice cracks a little and she continues. "I said I wanted him back, but there was nothing that could be done. I signed papers. My baby had already been adopted."

Wind scrapes the top of my head and a crow squawks four times — four for a boy, like maybe it knows what we're talking about. I think Miss Turner might cry, but she doesn't. Listening with a closed mouth isn't as easy as it sounds. The scariest part about the truth is facing the things you fear the most.

When Miss Turner gets back to the subject of Aunt Millie, I cringe just a little. I can't imagine her being kind and helpful the way Miss Turner described.

"It didn't take long to figure out that Millie hadn't a clue when it came to looking after babies." I would be laughing at that one if I weren't the baby she ended up looking after for real. "So they eventually put her to work in the laundry. She'd slip up to the nursery, though. I'd see her there most every day. She asked so many questions. She told me she was undercover and not to tell. I don't know what she expected to find out or why she just didn't come right out and ask the owners about her sister. I suppose she had her reasons, though. When I left she was still working there."

Undercover? Aunt Millie? That would have been a sight to behold, although it does sound more like the Aunt Millie I know — sneaking behind people's backs like that. At least she tried to find my mother, make her come back and do the right thing by me. Maybe Aunt Millie isn't the tough bird she makes herself out to be.

"That's all I know, Cammie, other than the letter I wrote."

"So I was born at a home for unwed mothers," I say, testing out the sound of this new information. Aunt Millie always told me I was born in the back seat of someone's car.

"That would be my guess. Girls were coming in all the time. Some hardly stayed a week. Some, like me, stayed for months. The Youngs insisted on privacy. We were warned not to talk about our time at the home. But Millie must have known something or she wouldn't have come there asking about her sister."

"But what about me? What did she do with me when she came there to work?" I only ever thought of Aunt Millie as a bootlegger, not someone with a regular job.

"She never mentioned you. Just her sister. All she asked about was her sister."

If I ever get to where I can figure Aunt Millie out, I could probably send for a certificate to hang on the wall and have myself declared a genius, because figuring her out will be as complicated as bringing about peace to the entire planet. And with all the fighting going on around the world, that will be a miracle through and through. When it comes to my life, and me trying to find out any of the particulars, she can string out a bunch of malarkey without batting an eye. Never mind that none of it's true. If I could tell lies as slick as Aunt Millie can, you can bet my life would have taken a whole other turn. Only what's the good of making up lies just to suit yourself?

Eventually, the truth comes out, and that's when the trouble always starts. I've had plenty of experience in that department, dealing with Aunt Millie over the years. But I'm slowly getting to the bottom of things. When Christmas comes, I'll get the whole truth and nothing but the truth. I won't stop pestering until I do. Right now Miss Turner's my ace in the hole. Just let Aunt Millie weasel her way out of this.

A scattering of brown leaves swirls along the ground and I shiver as the November air whips my legs. At this rate the trees will soon be bare, stretching their naked branches up to the sky, and there's something about it that seems a little sad. Nessa speaks up just then, like until that moment she didn't have anything important to say. She looks at me in a curious way.

"At least you've found another piece to the mystery," she says.

"What are you talking about, Nessa?"

"The mystery of Cammie Turple."

Me? A mystery? Maybe Nessa's right. Aunt Millie sure

has some explaining to do. Knowing her, she'll come up with a bunch of new lies to cover up the old ones just like she has in the past. Only this time I'll be armed with some facts. I have to wonder if any of this has something to do with the reason she doesn't want Ed to adopt me. With Aunt Millie it's impossible to speculate. One thing's for certain: The real story of Cammie Turple is a whole lot more complicated than I ever imagined.

Chapter Twenty-one

The music is already playing in the girls' gymnasium when we arrive. I'm feeling pretty snazzy in Nessa's green print dress tonight. The row of white eyelet on the hem swishes against my legs. Me, strutting along like nobody's business, about as dolled up as a Hollywood starlet for the night.

Last week, Nessa and Ellen brought in a bunch of dresses from home. There were plenty to choose from. Ellen's tastes are different from Nessa's: dark navies and deep reds, browns, and oranges that suit her complexion and dark brown hair; Nessa's about as light as anyone could get without using bleach. We spent an entire evening trying the dresses on, deciding what we liked and what looked best. I chose the green dress I saw in Nessa's closet the weekend of my birthday. Everyone said it was a good choice. Nessa's sporting the dress her mother bought her especially for the dance. It's blue with a white collar and has gathers in the front. Nessa's the luckiest duck in the whole school.

Deciding on an outfit was the easy part; knowing what to do if a boy asks me to dance will be a whole other thing. We helped Jennie and Rebecca pick out dresses because neither one of them can see at all. Rebecca has on the red and brown one from Ellen's stack.

"Do I look like a dream?" she asked, twirling around slowly.

"A dream come true," we assured her.

We all agreed that the yellow-and-white dress in Nessa's collection went nicely with Jennie's brown hair. I tied a white satin bow on top of her head when we were getting ready this evening. She asked me again if I was ready to write a verse in her autograph book. Each time someone writes a verse for Jennie, she sets it to memory. She even knows the colour of the page each person wrote on. "When I close my eyes, I can picture what the colours look like," she said, like everyone can remember things from when they were five.

"I'm still working on it," I said, straightening her hair ribbon so it wouldn't get lost in her curls. Everyone keeps giving me ideas but none of them feel right. I don't want to write about diaper pins and having twins or the ocean wearing rubber pants to keep its bottom dry — those things are all cute but they've got no meat to them. I've been hoping to come up with something no one else has written.

The necklace I'm wearing came from Greenburg's Department Store right here in the city. I keep feeling for the turquoise stone to make sure it's still there. Mrs. Maxwell took me to the store the day after my birthday, and Nessa helped me pick it out. Nearly two weeks since I bought it, it's the first time I've had some place fancy enough to wear it.

"Turquoise is the birthstone for December," Mrs. Maxwell said at the jewelry counter that day. I picked up each box that held a necklace in it. Seemed like the perfect thing to spend birthday money on. A card came from Ed with a crisp five-dollar bill the week before. I didn't open it until the third. The girls were impressed with my willpower.

The school doesn't make much of a deal out of birthdays, but neither did Aunt Millie when I was growing up. Usually there was a cake and sometimes she'd bake a few dimes inside it for me, but that was about it. When you're not used to a lot it doesn't take much to please you. Along with the card and money, there was a short note from Ed asking me how I'm doing and he hoped I was keeping my grades up. He signed off by telling me he could hardly wait for Christmas and maybe I would like to spend some time with him and Miranda. Miranda — I have to wonder what she thinks about this idea of Ed's. It's not like she's even met me. What if she doesn't want someone who can't see so well hanging around? I've been trying not to think about her too much. I've only ever thought of Ed loving my mother, even though she probably didn't deserve it. Something about him seeing someone else, someone he plans to spend the rest of his days with, feels strange.

I almost fell over when a parcel came from Aunt Millie the day after my birthday — some licorice whips (my favourite) and a pair of mittens she said she knit herself, like I'd believe that. Her note tickled my funny bone. The thought of Aunt Millie sitting in a rocking chair with knitting needles clicking together makes me want to laugh out loud.

I quickly make myself a promise not to let Aunt Millie into my head this evening. Tomorrow I'll be heading back to Tanner for the holidays. After that I'll deal with Aunt Millie. Tonight, I plan on having a time for myself.

"There are refreshments on the table," says Miss Turner as we walk into the gymnasium. I smile real big at her. It's like that day at the Public Gardens never happened. A month after the fact and she acts like it was no big deal, me thinking she was my mother of all things.

Nessa and I sashay on over, playing it cool until the dance actually gets underway. It's the one time of the year we're actually allowed to talk to the boys. No one wants to come off looking desperate, like it would be the end of the world if we didn't have someone ask us to dance.

I help myself to an egg sandwich even though I'm feeling a little unsettled. If I keep busy, maybe I won't have to worry about making it onto the dance floor. Dabbing my mouth with a napkin, I'm careful not to end up with egg stuck on my face. Nessa is wolfing down some of the sweets. Tammy reaches across me for a sandwich. Seconds later we're joined by Mary Louise and Amy. In no time flat, a cluster of girls is milling around the refreshments. Hands reach and take and the food starts to disappear from the plates.

"Where are the boys?" I ask, squinting and leaning in toward Nessa. You'd at least think they'd be somewhere near the food. No one's dancing. Maybe this whole thing will end up being a bust.

"They're standing by the wall," says Nessa, pointing across the room. "But don't worry. They're just waiting for someone to start."

The music is loud but then I suppose it would have to be with everyone talking and filling the room with noise. Nessa's scoping out the joint — trying to see Frankie

Parker from all the way across the room is my guess. I haven't a clue where Barry Huphman is, and I can't see well enough to pick him out from the crowd. I'm not even sure I want him to ask me for a dance. It would be a lot less pressure on me if he doesn't. I don't really know him, just the soft sound of his voice.

All Nessa's been talking about the last few weeks is Frankie Parker, speculating as to how many dances she'll have with him. Earlier in the week he called her on the pay phone and asked if she'd go steady with him. I guess now they're an item so long as they don't get caught.

The notes started flying back and forth Mrs. Christi's room about a week ago. No one wanted to end up standing around the food table with no one to dance with. You could have knocked me over with a feather when a note landed on my desk and it was actually for me. The boys sure have this whole note-tossing thing perfected. Mrs. Christi never suspected a thing. Later, in the dormitory, the girls oohed and aahed as I read what Barry Huphman wrote — nothing mushy, just that he'd like it if I saved a dance for him.

"Barry's one of the best dancers, and a real snake charmer," said Tammy, grinning from ear to ear.

When I complained that I didn't know how to dance, Nessa said she'd teach me.

"Barry's danced with all of us…but he never wrote any notes before," said Jennie. "I wonder what that means?" Me, I couldn't help but smile at that news, thinking maybe it's possible that one of the boys might actually like me.

We'd practiced our dance steps in the recreation room every spare chance we had. We danced along to Kitty Wells, Hank Williams, and Patti Page — whatever happened to be playing on the radio. When my feet wouldn't do what I wanted them to, Nessa told me to follow her lead.

"Stop looking down," she said. When I'd bring my head up she'd remind me not to stomp on her feet. Being about as graceful as a cow on ice doesn't make you a good dancing partner. I didn't think I'd ever get the knack of it. But then I dug in those Turple heels of mine and got determined.

"If someone doesn't soon start dancing, I'm marching over there and grabbing Frankie by the hand," says Nessa, chomping on what looks to be another date square.

"You will not!" gasps Mary Louise, trying to sound tough, which isn't easy seeing how tiny she is. "I'll drag you back myself," she adds without cracking a grin. As if! I want to laugh. No one's afraid of a runt.

Eventually, some of the boys get some backbone and come across the room. My heart patters. Still pretending to survey the food table, I'm as afraid of being asked to dance as I am of not being asked. What if I end up standing by the sandwiches all evening long? Cammie Turple, the biggest wallflower at school.

And then, like a star that shoots across the night sky, I feel a hand on my shoulder.

"Can I have this dance?" says a soft voice behind me. I turn around, smiling. Dirty blonde hair — I never would have guessed. The smile on Barry Huphman's face leaps out at me. There's no way I can refuse. We walk out onto the dance floor, my knees a tiny bit wobbly. His hands are as soft and warm as a cat lying in the afternoon sun. He smells like sunshine, too. My feet are heavy, my legs as stiff as a pair of stilts as I try to keep up with him. I remember the things Nessa taught me: don't look down at the floor; don't step on your partner's feet. Glide…glide. One and two and three and four.

After the first few dances my knees start working without me telling them to. I dance with Barry and everyone else who asks. Soft hands, hard hands, and even the ones covered in warts. Just look at me, Cammie Turple. I never would have thought dancing could be so much fun.

About halfway through the evening I head back over to the refreshment table. This dancing business sure makes you thirsty. I take a paper cup and Miss Turner pours me some juice. "Having fun?" she asks. And me, I'm beaming inside like the first star at night.

Sipping my juice, I reach for the stone on my necklace and rub it between my fingers. Feeling like I've got the world by the tail, I can't help smiling when Miss Turner says, "What a pretty necklace you have, Cammie." I've always wanted a necklace of my own. I used to sneak into Aunt Millie's room and try hers on.

"Thank you," I say in a polished voice, mostly because this whole evening has been perfect so far and I can't imagine anything messing it up. "I got it at Greenburg's. It's my birthstone."

"Oh, dear," says Miss Turner, her voice filled to the brim with pity. "Emerald is the birthstone for May. You bought the wrong one."

"But May's not my birthday, Miss Turner." I'm shocked that she could have forgotten something like that. Especially since her baby was born around the same time as me. I've heard tell of people's memories going out from under them, but Miss Turner's too young for that. "My birthday was just the other week," I remind her, not that she was on duty that day.

"This doesn't make sense," she says, her blonde curls bouncing as she shakes her head.

I down the last of my juice. I know how Cinderella must have felt when she went to the ball. Who will be the next one to ask me for a dance? "Tennessee Waltz" starts playing and I'm burning to get back onto the dance floor. I wish Miss Turner would stop talking.

"I was there in May," Miss Turner continues. "That's when Millie came looking for her sister, not December. Brenda had her baby sometime in May. I'm positive."

A strange feeling shimmies up my spine. My brain goes a little wonky like I just jumped headfirst into ice-cold water. The noise in the gymnasium fades for a second and then returns. The empty cup I'm holding suddenly weighs a hundred pounds. Miss Turner pries it from my bent fingers and sets it on the table.

"Come on, Cammie," says Nessa, hurrying over and grabbing my hand. "I love this song." As Nessa pulls me along with her, I look back at Miss Turner standing at the table all by herself. I want to slip to the floor and melt away.

Chapter Twenty-two

The countryside goes by and I can't quite figure out if I'm going toward Tanner or away from Halifax. Somehow neither one seems quite right. Bare trees and blue skies; the sun winks at me through the window of the train. The fields look yellow and old, like they're suddenly tired of fall. The train clacks down the tracks and I almost forgot how loud it is. I try concentrating on the scenery, but emptying your head isn't like dumping your chamber pail in the morning. Hard to keep the thoughts from filling your head back up. Nessa's right. Everything about my life is a mystery.

Last night's dance feels like a stale doughnut, something you'd still like to bite into even though you know it won't taste very good. The dance itself was fun, but I can't stop thinking about what Miss Turner said: that I was born in May, not December. After the dance, she apologized for stirring things up.

"I should have left well enough alone," she said, sounding like she could trip over her bottom lip if she wasn't careful. But I'm glad for this new information even though things keep getting more and more complicated. "I'm sure there's a simple explanation for it all," she added.

"Do you really think so?" I asked. But she didn't answer.

If I'm right about those papers in Aunt Millie's jewelry box, I can settle this thing once and for all. Case closed. Ed can adopt me and I'll be on my way. Makes me wonder what the holidays will be like *this* year. Not like Christmas has ever been anything special, except for the fact that Aunt Millie wouldn't let anyone come in to have a drink. But when New Year's Eve hit, watch out! The whole crew would land there. Glasses would be clinking together, shotguns lighting up the sky, hooting and hollering, the likes you'd never see the rest of the year.

"Right here's the best spot in Tanner to be ringing in the New Year," she'd squeal, like it pleased her all to pieces to think hers was *the* place to be every December 31st. Likely now that she and Drew are back together he'll be having something to say about that, unless he's all up for celebrating, too. It's not like I'm going to lose sleep wondering about it, though. So long as I get what I'm after, that's all I care about. Aunt Millie isn't the only one who can do undercover work. I'll gain her trust, maybe even make it seem like I don't want Ed to adopt me after all, and the first chance I get I'll hightail it for those papers. Once Ed has my birth records we can get this show on the road.

Ed's waiting at the train station in his old green truck. At least one adult in my life keeps promises. Aunt Millie always says Ed is irresponsible, but that couldn't be further from the truth. He takes my bag from me and swings it over his shoulder. He rubs my head like he did the day he came to the school and tells me I'm getting tall. My knees go a little wobbly on me when I realize that there's someone sitting in the truck. I can only imagine it must be Miranda. I haul in a deep breath and climb in.

Her dark brown hair sticks out from beneath her cap and the lipstick she's wearing is bright red. She smells like the pressed powder Aunt Millie wears when she goes out on the town. Taking my hand in hers, she says, "It's nice to finally meet you, Cammie. Ed talks about you all the time." I make a strange sound that doesn't even resemble a laugh. I can't stop staring at Miranda. She has the prettiest smile I've ever seen. I don't ever want to look away.

We gab all the way to Tanner as if it's the most natural thing, like chewing bubble gum or gnawing through a licorice whip. I can't imagine I was ever worried about meeting Miranda. Ed tells us the same story about hitchhiking to Yarmouth and nearly eating his way through a fifty-pound bag of potatoes. I laugh with Miranda like I'm hearing the story for the first time. I can tell Ed is pleased. Miranda asks if I'm learning Braille. I explain to her that we have large-print books at the school and that I can even see regular print when I take my glasses off and hold things up close. I don't mind her asking. Most people don't know what it's like not to be able to see so well, but they're afraid to ask you anything about it. Evelyn was never afraid to ask. That's one thing I always appreciated.

"My hands can't make sense of all those dots," I explain, but then I tell her about Jennie and how she can read Braille faster than those of us who read printed words.

Just before we turn down the Lake Ridge Road toward Tanner, Ed gets serious. "I don't think Millie will let me come in, so I guess you'll be on your own when we get there." He takes one hand off the wheel and rubs the back of his neck. "She's not too happy with me these days."

For a time all I hear is a soft pattering inside the truck. Stealing a glance over at Ed, I can make out him tapping the steering wheel. Ed only taps when he's antsy about something.

"Don't worry, Ed. I can handle Aunt Millie." I'll proceed with caution; that much I know. It's best not to ruffle her feathers. She'll just put on her crow face and that's never a pretty sight.

"Have you had time to think about what we talked about? Me, I mean *us*, adopting you — the three of us being a family someday? We'd give you a good home."

"I've been thinking about it a lot lately."

"But you haven't made up your mind — is that it?" Could be I hear a hint of disappointment in his voice, or maybe it's just wishful thinking on my part.

Sorry, Ed, but I can't agree to anything until I've solved the mystery of me.

"I'm not making any promises right now," I say, climbing out of the truck. Things are too complicated at the moment, me hardly knowing a thing about when and where I was born. I can't let him get his hopes up real big just to let them collapse. I've had enough experience in that department.

I'm back to square one with Aunt Millie. It's not like I can ask her to come clean. I've tried that a gazillion times in the past and it never got me anywhere. Getting to the truth with Aunt Millie will be like panning for gold, sifting out all the sand and rocks, hoping to find the tiniest nugget at the bottom. But all this is about my life, and unravelling this mystery. Who better to do it than me?

Chapter Twenty-three

Tanner is different. I feel it the moment I step out of Ed's truck. Or maybe it's me having been gone these months, life continuing on without me. Like maybe I don't count anymore. You go away and expect everything to be waiting for you just the way you left it — all the clouds and blades of grass, the trees and even the air. Nothing ever stays the same. Change sneaks up on you like a snake in the grass, and when it finally catches up to you, you want to let out a scream.

Aunt Millie meets me in the doorway, and if I didn't know better I'd say she's happy to see me.

"Look at you, Cammie Turple. What a sight for sore eyes you are. Drew...Drew," she calls, looking over her shoulder, "it's Cammie all the way back from the city. Hey — your hair's short," she squawks when I take off my tam. She ushers me in and peels off my coat like I've been gone for years instead of a few months. Drew is leaning against the doorjamb like he could care less. Looks like he's snarling unless what I'm seeing is a smile he's forcing out for Aunt Millie's sake.

"How's it going?" he asks like he gives two hoots, and I say, "Okay," because that's all the answer I can squeeze out for the time being. Once the pleasantries are over, he doesn't hang around, which suits me fine and dandy. I don't much want Drew Bordmann in my space if I can help it.

Aunt Millie keeps clacking away like she can't get the words out of her fast enough. What's the school like? Are the meals any good? Do I have a best friend? Are the teachers any good? Am I staying out of trouble? She pays close attention to what I'm saying but she doesn't fool me. When sweet and nice comes out of Aunt Millie there's usually a reason. My answers are short and to the point. I'm ready to pounce the moment she brings Ed into the picture. Just let her criticize him and see what happens. Except she doesn't say a thing about Ed or the adoption, not a peep.

Pushing a plate of food in front of me, she tells me to eat up. "Beef stew — your favourite. I even made chocolate cake." I have to admit Aunt Millie *is* a good cook, even though I know she's trying to butter me up. Seeing how I haven't eaten since breakfast this morning, I dig in. She sits watching like maybe I'll disappear if she doesn't. I don't know what to make of this new version of Aunt Millie. Could be now that she's retired from bootlegging she doesn't know what to do with herself. Maybe she needs to find herself a hobby. Just as long as I'm not that hobby.

"We're heading into Sheppard Square. Drew's going to cut a tree on the way home," she says after I've swallowed down every last bite. "Want to come along?" Excuse me for being suspicious, but never before has Aunt Millie invited me to go anywhere with her and Drew. Never.

"I'm kind of tired. Think I'll take a nap while you're gone."

Seconds before she heads out the door, Aunt Millie stops. "We've got things to discuss later — me and you. Sometime when Drew's not around." She pauses before adding, "I suppose you'll want to visit that Merry boy while you're home."

As soon as Drew's truck heads up the road I put on my coat and hat and tear out the back door. I'm dying to look for my birth records, but Evelyn has to come first. Him ending up in the hospital was my fault. If it hadn't been for me he wouldn't have blown up Hux Wagner's moonshine still in the first place.

Evelyn knows I'm coming home today, I told him so in my last letter. Maybe he'll be waiting for me like all those

times in the past. I race toward our secret camp down by
the river, my feet slapping against the ground, hopeful in
a way I haven't felt in months. Our camp might only be a
clearing in the bushes, but we spent some of our best times
there, making plans and chewing the fat. Just because I've
got a whole other life in the city doesn't mean I'll give up
on Evelyn.

I scurry down the path to the river, letting my feet lead
the way. I haven't felt this free for months. The trees, the
grass, the land, all look dead; the middle of December and
not a smidge of snow to whiten things up. Stepping inside
our camp, I shiver. All the secrets Evelyn and me shared,
all the plans we concocted — our disappointments and
victories and even tears — I can feel it all.

The wind whistles up across the river, and I think about
the day I almost drowned. How Jim Merry jumped in
the water and saved me. I used to think he was nothing
but a drunk and a bully. Funny how your opinion about
someone can change over time. Too bad most times those
circumstances have to be dire for any of that to happen. At
least Jim's not drinking anymore, but while he is trying to
make it up to Evelyn as best he can, it's not always easy to
forgive and forget the past.

The bottles and jars inside our camp are still lined up on
the board where we left them. The bricks are stacked on top

of one another. I count them. Eleven. Same as the day I left. Opening the cold cream jar, I look in at the blue eggshell Evelyn put inside for safekeeping. I touch it gently with the tip of my finger before screwing the top back on. Reaching into the tin, I take out our playing cards and shuffle them a few times.

The camp feels deserted, like time stopped the day I went away and forgot to start moving again, like ghosts from the past are waiting to jump out and grab me. The branches inside the camp tremble in the breeze. I'll wait for Evelyn a little longer. Hard to say how long Aunt Millie will be gone. I might have time to look for those papers yet.

Hearing my name, I spin around. "Evelyn!" I gasp, looking out through the doorway. The wind answers with a breeze too fragile to hold the tiniest sound. Imagination can play funny tricks on you. Maybe he's busy with Spark and doesn't want to leave. Outside I put my feet though the old tire, grab on tight, and start swinging.

I wait for as long as I dare. Looking down along the river's black water, I head back home, dragging my disappointment with me like an old wet blanket. It was stupid of me to come here. I should have known better. Hope doesn't always make sense, but sometimes it's the only thing you have.

—

As darkness closes in for the evening, I creep up the

steps in my stocking feet, slipping across the polished floorboards like a skater on a frozen pond. Aunt Millie and Drew are in the kitchen playing whist. They'll be there for hours like they have been the past few nights. Finding an ounce of privacy has been next to impossible with Aunt Millie hovering around like a hummingbird to hollyhocks, inviting me to help decorate the tree and make fruitcake — as if she's ever let me do any of these things in the past. She's about as genuine as a three-dollar bill.

"No sense being a stick in the mud," she said, so I helped her with the fruitcake this afternoon to keep her off my back.

The door to Aunt Millie's room is open a crack. I push on it and enter. Reaching for the pull chain, I snap the light on. Below me, Aunt Millie lets out a squeal. Drew's gravelly voice rumbles. I head toward her dresser, to the wooden box where she keeps her jewelry, careful not to step on any squeaky floorboards. If the letter isn't there I'm not sure where I'll look next. But I'll worry about all that later.

I take a big breath and open the lid, my fingers tingling like they suddenly fell asleep. Digging through the mound of jewelry, I pull out a bunch of metal — chains and brooches and earrings twined together like worms in a tin can. My fingertips butt against some paper in the bottom of the box. It's still there!

Setting my glasses on the dresser, I hold the envelope up close. My hands tremble with excitement. This has to be it!

The envelope looks all official: *To: Mildred Turple.* Aunt Millie never keeps anything. It has to be important. Straightening out the letter, I commence reading. The words don't make sense at first. My head starts to spin as I work my way to the bottom of the page.

Regret to inform you...Complications from childbirth...a girl, stillborn...burial.

A cold sensation trickles over me, filling my shoes, and I can't stop shivering.

"What are you doing in my room?" asks Aunt Millie, only the words come out in bubbles, like she's got her head under water. I take a sudden gulp of air and turn around so slowly I'm hardly sure I'm moving at all. Maybe I'm not. Maybe I'm stuck between the past and the present with no place to call home. The letter slips out of my hands and flutters to the floor. Aunt Millie makes a nosedive toward it and snaps it up.

"Cammie, what did you do?" The fact that she doesn't even sound mad frightens me the most. My knees want to crumple but I force them not to bend. My tongue can't straighten out all the words that are in my head to say.

Every fear, every bit of anger, every worry I've ever felt sits like a rock in my stomach and I can't move.

"You weren't supposed to find out like this," she says.

Chapter Twenty-four

May 15, 1940
The Ideal Maternity Home
East Chester, Nova Scotia

Dear Miss Turple,

It is with deepest regret that I must inform you of the death of your sister, Brenda, on May 8th of this year, due to complications from childbirth. The child, a girl, was stillborn. Please know that everything medically possible was done to save both mother and child, but some things are left in God's hands. As mere mortals there is little we can do to intervene when something is not part of God's will.

Since immediate attempts to locate her next of kin proved futile, we here at the home were forced to step up and take charge. Therefore, both mother and child were laid to rest in Fox Point Cemetery, according to your sister's wishes shortly before her passing. Please know that your dearly departed sister spoke highly of you during her stay here with us and it was her wish for you not to suffer unduly by her death.

There is another matter pertaining to the business side of your sister's care at the Ideal Maternity Home. In accordance with the legal contract your sister signed upon entering the home, there is the matter of $400 owing, to cover her stay here as well as burial fees for both of the deceased. Your immediate attention to this matter would be greatly appreciated. Please remit payment to the above address as soon as possible to preserve your sister's good name even in death. Everyone deserves a second chance.

Yours in God,

Lila Young

Drew comes upstairs to see what's going on. Aunt Millie barks at him to scram. He must know we've got some serious business to discuss because he doesn't kick up a stink about being ordered to leave.

"You might want to sit down for this," Aunt Millie says, but I stand with my feet firmly planted. I'm tough. I can take whatever she has to say.

"Just give me the facts. No sugar-coating. I'm not a little kid anymore."

I listen to everything Aunt Millie has to say, how she went to that home for unwed mothers to find out what happened to her sister. Aunt Millie, undercover — the idea sounds just as ridiculous as it did the first time Miss Turner said it.

When Aunt Millie gets through talking, she asks me why I've got nothing to say. But what's there to say when you find out your entire life has been one gigantic lie after another? Then it hits me like a load of bricks: All this means that Ed's not my father. That sends a spike of disappointment through me.

"It's really not so bad, not like you think," she says. "You were born at that maternity home just like Brenda's baby."

"Not so bad! You've got to be kidding. What about all the lies you told? All the time I spent wondering why my mother never came." Spite starts climbing up my backbone. All the lies Aunt Millie told — it was to save her own skin.

"I just took what really happened and rearranged it a teensy bit. It seemed simple at the time. Someone had to take you."

"You mean *you* adopted me?" I ask, finally getting a grip. When Aunt Millie tells a story there are always pieces missing, not to mention the parts that don't make any real sense.

"Not exactly."

"What do you mean, not exactly?" If I don't soon get to the bottom of all of this, I'll blow my stack. Guaranteed.

"There was that matter of a bill owing. I couldn't tell her who I really was. She'd be after her money. But I also knew you were one of the ones who wouldn't be adopted — not with your eyes. When I brought you back to Tanner I told everyone you were Brenda's. No one knew the difference. I guess over time I started to believe it myself. You have her colouring. I think that's why I took to you like I did. As far as anyone knew, you could have been Brenda's baby."

"But you told me she'd be back one day. You said she was off making her mark. You let me hate her. You're nothing but a liar! A big fat liar!" The words are bunching up on me, pushing against my cheeks and tongue.

"We all need something to believe in, Cammie. No one wanted Brenda to come home more than me. I thought you'd eventually give up waiting."

"You thought I'd give up? Like it wasn't important?" Fury forms a ball inside me. Twelve years of hope and longing finally let loose. "You could be lying now for all I know!" I scream at the top of my lungs. Grabbing my glasses, I push out past her. I haven't got time for more of her lies.

"Go ask Jim Merry if you don't believe me," she says. I stop and spin around. She has my attention. "He was there the night I brought you home. We left in his wagon when the freighters came through. He went to Chester with barrels and came home with a baby. But then Ed had to go and ruin everything by showing up here after the war. Why couldn't he have gone someplace else to live? Why did he have to come back to Sheppard Square? Why did he have to find out about you?"

I scowl and give Aunt Millie a look. "None of this is Ed's fault." Ed — I've got to tell Ed. It's only fair. But what's he going to say? Guess I can kiss this adoption thing goodbye. Maybe he'll be relieved. Maybe the whole idea was Ed just doing his fatherly duty. Now he'll be free. Could be it'll make him happy not to have a twelve-year-old kid with bad eyes on his hands.

"My real parents?" I give a sniff but only because I'm done feeling sorry for myself. It's time to be tough. Like it or lump it, this is my life. No more lies to protect the truth.

"There's no way of knowing that. 'People only adopt the perfect babies.' That's what Mrs. Young said one day. 'Mix some water and molasses,' she said. 'That baby's not going to live anyway.' The old bat was talking about you, Cammie. And, well, a baby can't live on molasses and water. Even I knew that. I never did find out what happened to Brenda, but I sure as heck couldn't leave you there, not after the things I heard."

Scurrying to her closet, Aunt Millie pulls out a scrapbook and pitches it open on the bed. "Right here," she says, tapping a finger onto the page. I get in close to see. The page is filled with newspaper clippings with titles like: "Couple Found Not Guilty," "Controversy Surrounding Home for Unwed Mothers," "Babies for Sale?" I flip the pages. More articles.

"I started saving everything I could find in case any of this came back on me. The old battleaxe kept sending letters, wanting her money, threatening to get the law involved, but I knew she wouldn't do that. Not after what was in these articles. It's a good thing she didn't know who I really was when I went there to work."

"But my parents…." I'm back to square one in that department.

"Forget your parents, Cammie. They gave you up. I'm the one who wanted you."

For all my life I only ever wanted to hear someone to say that. I never in a million years believed it would be Aunt Millie.

Chapter Twenty-five

The full moon reaches its fingers through the tree branches and grabs at the furniture in my bedroom. I sit on the floor looking out at it, wondering why life has to be so complicated. Why can't it be as simple as a morning sunrise, or a moonbeam in the dead of night? I can still hear Aunt Millie's words in my head like the scorch marks from a hot iron: *Go ask Jim Merry if you don't believe me.* All these years she wanted nothing to do with Jim Merry. She said it was because he was a drunk and a bully, but that's not all true. She trusted him in the past, but that was before his son died and he started drinking on account of it.

"*Loose lips sink ships*— a promise doesn't mean much to a drunk," Aunt Millie continued. "I kept thinking he'd shoot his mouth off. I'd get sent off to jail and then where would you be — tell me that? Back at that home, slowly starving to death, that's where."

Around and around the story goes, clunking along like a flat tire on a pickup truck. I can't make my head stop thinking.

"All I wanted was a little part of her, Cammie. That's all I wanted. Brenda was all I had, my only sister. You were the closest thing I could get. And you needed someone, too."

—

I go to see Evelyn the next day because there's no one else I can tell all this to, and I've got to let it out before I split wide open.

When the Merrys' front door swings open, I'm not prepared to see Jim Merry standing on the other side. I thought he'd be out in the barn doing chores, not sitting around the house answering knocks at his front door. I push the fruitcake I'm holding at him and say, "Aunt Millie sent this," like he's not going to notice her sudden generosity.

"It's Christmas," Aunt Millie had said when I gave her a queer look. "We're supposed to do nice things, aren't we? Goodwill toward everyone and all that. No need to look at me like I've lost my mind, Cammie. I can do nice things, too, you know. No one ever gives me a chance."

"Ethel," calls Jim behind his shoulder. "It's the little blind girl from up the road." I stand in the porch like the cat's got my tongue. There's nothing I want to say to Jim

Merry — other than I'm glad he finally got around to getting Evelyn the sloop ox he's wanted since forever and a day. Knowing me it would come out sounding snotty, so I keep quiet. "Back from the city for the holidays?" he asks. I nod. No real answer required and I'm glad for that.

"Evelyn will be happy you're here," says Mrs. Merry, wiping her hands on her apron as she heads my way. "We've been wondering when you'd come — haven't we, Jim?"

Leaving my boots in the porch, I follow behind Mrs. Merry in my stocking feet. I'm feeling a little antsy. There's so much to say, I'm not sure where to start. Evelyn's probably not going to want to hear about the trouble I've been having coming up with the right verse for Jennie's autograph book, and I know he's not going to give a flying fig about our Christmas dance because he always said dancing was stupid. Church? Forget it. I'm not sure he's ever stepped inside one. He'd be interested in hearing about the tramcars in Halifax, the Public Gardens, and our trips to the Stadacona Base for swimming, but I put all those things in the letters I wrote. I don't want to bore him.

When my legs won't take me any farther, I stop right outside the room. I'd planned it out in my head last night sitting in the moonlight, how I'd rush to Evelyn's side and start blabbing away. So much for well-thought-out plans. Mrs. Merry marches across the room and says, "Evelyn…

Cammie's here." She turns back toward me and tells me to come in. She's smiling like it's made her day to have me come visit and that thought sticks in my throat just a little. I should have come way before now, but some things aren't as easy as they seem.

I move across the room slow, like I'm walking through water. It's been so long since I've seen Evelyn, maybe he'll think I've gone on with my life without giving him any consideration when, really, I think of him most every day. That's what best friends do. Pulling in a deep breath, I let go of these past three months, dissolve them in my mind like a hailstone in July, and hurry toward him. Evelyn Merry, that thick mop of brown hair, is a sight for sore eyes. I can't stop grinning.

Giving him a quick nudge on the arm I say, "You're never going to believe this." I squeeze his hand and picture a smile on his face like he's trying to hold it in. Settling my rump into the cushioned chair beside him, I pretend that I haven't been gone away, and the words start flowing out of me. I regurgitate the whole incident like a cow bringing up its cud, careful so as not to leave out any of the juicy details. I tell him about the letter I found in Aunt Millie's jewelry box while looking for my birth record, how Aunt Millie's sister never was my mother, that she died along with her baby at a maternity home. I tell him how I was a baby in the nursery with umpteen other babies, waiting for someone to adopt me, only no one wanted a baby with bad eyes. And I tell him how Aunt Millie took a job at the home to find out what really happened to her sister.

"Imagine Aunt Millie with a respectable job," I say with a quick laugh. I know this tickles him just as much as it does me.

I go on to say how Aunt Millie went to that home to get to the truth but ended up coming home with me. I work my way through all the particulars like I'm never going to shut up. I tell him that Aunt Millie brought me home with her because she wanted me, really wanted me, and the words bunch up on me like when you swallow a gulp of water too fast.

"Ed won't be adopting me because he's not even my father," I say, throwing my hands up in the air. I tell Evelyn about the newspaper articles Aunt Millie saved over the years about the people running that maternity home, waiting for him to come out with something smart the way he sometimes does. I keep on gibbering like a lone bird singing into the wind. Then I whisper to him how his own pa was the one who helped Aunt Millie bring me home to Tanner.

"Imagine that," I say. "It's like we were bound to be best friends right from the start." My hands press together and

I wait for Evelyn to say something like how everything kind of makes sense now, and that finally the pieces all fit together. If only I could make a big smile spread across his face.

"Evelyn..." I stop. The rest of what I want to say won't move past my front teeth. My words have come to a screeching halt and all that's left is air. The silence hurts my ears and I want to scream. I hate that he won't speak to me.

But then Mrs. Merry walks into the room.

"Thanks for coming, Cammie. Your letters have meant so much. We read them every day."

Blinking a few times to hold in the tears, I thank her for the letters she sent, too.

"I like reading about Spark," I say. Getting up off my chair, I start buttoning my coat and pull my tam down over my head. I'm stopped in my tracks when Mrs. Merry starts talking again.

"He could wake up any time, you know — that's what the doctor says. They really don't know why he hasn't, what's keeping him asleep." She smoothes the wrinkles out of the sheets on Evelyn's bed. "He opens his eyes for hours at a time, but he can't quite wake up. It's like he's in some other world...but you'll come back, won't you, Evelyn?" she says, leaning in close to him. She straightens back up and adds,

"They didn't want me to bring him home, but I can look after him here. Home is the best place to be."

I listen for the sound of doubt in her voice but don't hear it. Six months and even I'm afraid to keep hoping. I guess if your ma gives up on you it's time to call it quits. Evelyn has never been a quitter. I take a deep breath. Mrs. Merry hasn't given up hope, and neither will I. Reaching for the door latch, I turn around.

"Evelyn's a real fighter. I bet he's going to wake up soon," I say right before I leave.

Chapter Twenty-six

Christmas songs are playing on the radio. Aunt Millie's belting them out as if she can carry a decent tune. She promises popcorn but I tell her to forget it. Can't she tell I've got things on my mind? Even the doctor doesn't know why Evelyn's still asleep. I don't know what I was expecting. If all the juicy details of my life didn't wake him up, then I don't know what will. At least when I was in Halifax, sending letters to him, I could dream up in my head that he was awake, that he and his pa were breaking in that sloop of his. But seeing him just lying in bed is the worst thing imaginable.

Grabbing Aunt Millie by the hand, Drew pulls her to her feet. They dance to "I've Got My Love To Keep Me Warm." It's pretty corny, Drew making over Aunt Millie like she's the woman of his dreams. Excuse me for not being sociable. The way Aunt Millie strung everyone along to save her own skin, letting me spend my life hoping for something that was never going to happen, is enough to make an angel swear. Then there's Ed, an innocent bystander. I'm not sure how he'll take the news. Under the right circumstances I might have felt grateful to know that Aunt Millie took me out of that horrible place, but lies that big don't go away the moment you decide to tell the truth.

There are presents under the tree. Three of them have my name on them. I snuck a peek earlier in the day when Drew and Aunt Millie were out in the kitchen. There's only one thing I want for Christmas. I'd pass up a lifetime of presents to hear Evelyn Merry say my name.

When a knock comes to the back door, Aunt Millie takes off.

"Hold your pickle," she says, dropping Drew's hand and marching out to the kitchen. Seems strange, someone coming to visit on Christmas Eve. Used to be a knock at the back door only meant one thing: one of the gang was coming by for a drink of moonshine. Aunt Millie assures me those days are long gone. I say time will tell.

"Cammie…it's for you!" Aunt Millie sounds like she's got a bee in her bonnet. I find out why the moment Ed's voice echoes in the background. Making a beeline for the kitchen, I wonder what Ed's doing here on Christmas Eve when he knows Aunt Millie's still perturbed with him.

"I got you a present," he says, shoving something brown and fuzzy into my arms. "I saw it in Bridgewater." I look into its round beady eyes, at the bright red ribbon around its neck. It's kind of cute, even though I'm probably too big for a teddy bear. I never had one growing up. Nessa has a whole shelf full of dolls but that's different. Even grown-ups collect dolls. My face suddenly drops. How am I going to tell Ed he's not my father?

"I knew it. You don't like it. I told Miranda you were too old," he says, rubbing the back of his neck.

"It's not that…. You should come in. I've got something to tell you."

"Do you think I dare? I mean, Millie…"

Looking behind my shoulder I see Aunt Millie give a nod. She turns and leaves, giving us some privacy. I listen for the sound of her shoes to get fainter before saying to Ed, "You might want to sit down for this."

"So, there you have it," I say once I've rehashed the whole thing for Ed. I squeeze the stuffed bear. "You're not really my father so you won't have to adopt me. We're not even related."

I wait for Ed to break the silence. It's hard to imagine what could be going through his mind. Pushing the teddy bear at him, I say, "You can take it with you."

Ed clears his throat. I expect he'll make some lame excuse and be on his way.

"Keep it," he says, clearing his throat, "unless you don't want it, that is."

"I just thought…." There go the words, bunching up on me again.

"You thought what?"

My chair suddenly becomes uncomfortable on the backside.

"Everything's different now. This…changes things." I catch myself kicking at the floor and stop.

"Changes what?" Ed practically barks at me.

"You don't have to adopt me." It should be pretty obvious without me having to spell it out for him.

"Have to? I never *had to*…did you ever stop to think I might actually *want* to adopt you?"

"Not really," I say with a peculiar laugh that only comes out when the nerves gang up on me.

"I don't see how this has to change anything. You don't have any parents. Miranda and I can still adopt you." I make a quick calculation of this, but before I can say anything Aunt Millie steps into the conversation.

"I already told you, Ed Hanover, Cammie's mine. You can't have her. I can't turn my back for a minute, can I?"

"And maybe you don't have any say about it," says Ed,

now jumping up off his chair. "Cammie's twelve. I'd say that's old enough to decide for herself."

"I've had her from the start, Ed. Right from the start. You come waltzing in here a few years ago and think you can turn everything upside down. Well, it doesn't work that way."

"With nothing legal, I say she's up for grabs," says Ed raising his voice.

Up for grabs? I'm not some prize to be drawn for at the New Ross fair.

"Hey!" I squawk, but no one pays attention.

The two of them start squabbling over me like I'm the last licorice whip in the jar at Mae Cushion's store. Then Drew joins in the racket — taking Aunt Millie's side and telling Ed he's got no rights at all. I tell them to quiet down but no one hears, not Ed or Drew, and certainly not Aunt Millie, who's now standing on a chair in the middle of the kitchen, shaking her fist in the air. There's more noise in the kitchen than there ever was when Aunt Millie was bootlegging and no one's even drinking.

"What do *you* want, Cammie?" asks Ed, suddenly turning toward me. "Who do you want to adopt you?"

My brain goes numb as Ed's question shoots through me. There were times when I might have answered right away, but now that I'm actually faced with the decision I don't know what I want.

"That's not fair, Ed," Aunt Millie squeals. "You've got no right."

"Neither do you." Before I have time to say anything they're back to their squabbling again.

A rattling sound behind me catches my attention. I never thought I'd be so happy to hear someone banging at the back door. Maybe whoever it is can talk some sense into the three of them. I hurry and lift the latch. Ed's question follows me. The wind pulls the latch from my hands and the door bangs against the house, bringing their squabbling to a sudden halt.

"What the devil are you doing here on Christmas Eve?" barks Aunt Millie, climbing down from her perch.

I can tell from the height and the clothes, and the way he's standing, that it's Jim Merry. He comes through the door, bringing an armful of cold air with him.

"Evelyn…" he manages to get out.

Not Evelyn, I want to cry out. *Not on Christmas! Not on any day!* I can't bear to hear what he's going to say to next.

"What about Evelyn?" Even Aunt Millie's voice is shaky. Jim looks around the room.

"He's awake," he croaks. "Evelyn's awake. He wants to see you. He wants to see you now, Cammie. Can you come?"

—

"I…was…with…Beecher," Evelyn says when it's just the two of us in his bedroom. His words come out slow. But I'm patient. I'll sit here all night if I have to.

"Your bother? But you were only a baby when he, you know…." It's too weird to say the word "died" out loud.

He swallows and blinks his eyes. "I didn't…know right away. I…I…thought he was…just a…a…kid…but then he…he told me who he was." Evelyn's voice isn't much more than a whisper.

"Maybe it was a dream," I say. "I mean, you did hurt your head."

Closing his eyes, he keeps talking. "Pa…Pa was there, but he…he didn't know me. Like…I was in the past. But… how? It was…so mixed up."

"We've all been so worried, Evelyn. Everyone in Tanner and Sheppard Square. We've all been hoping you'd wake up!"

He closes his eyes and I wait for what he has to say next. He shakes his head. "I was…with him…I…I…was with Beecher…And…" He swallows. "Pa was nice."

"He *is* nice. Ever since you got hurt. Your pa stopped drinking. He's a new man, Evelyn! Everyone says so. You did it. You got your pa to change. And that steer you've always wanted, he's standing in the pasture waiting for you. He'll make a good sloop ox once you get him broke," I say, like I know what I'm talking about when it comes to cattle.

Evelyn looks up from the bed and gives me a lopsided grin. No one can imagine how many times I've dreamed up that smile of Evelyn's in my head.

A peculiar look spreads across his face right before he says, "You be...believe me, C...Cammie, don't you — about Beecher?"

And I have no choice but to nod my head. When your best friend wakes up from a six-month sleep and tells you he's been with his dead brother this whole time, the only thing you can do is believe him.

Chapter Twenty-seven

Ed gabs all the way to the train station in Kentville like words are going out of style. He talks about all the things we'll do once the school year is over.

"There are some places I'd like to show you. Have you been to the ocean?"

"I've never been much of anywhere."

"We'll have to change that when you come home for the summer," he says, smiling. He promises Miranda will write to me every week. "I'm not much for letter-writing myself, but Miranda sure is."

At the train station he rubs my head before I step onto the platform. "You're sure about your decision?" he says. "It's not too late to change your mind. Miranda and I can petition the courts."

"I'm sure...at least for now," I say looking over at him. "How about you?"

"So long as Millie keeps up her end of things," he says. "Four weeks in the summer and some time over the Christmas break."

"That's what she promised," I say, nodding in agreement. "And we've got something on her now." Aunt Millie being the least bit co-operative, now that's something I could never have dreamed up.

"There won't be anything written down," says Ed.

"I don't need papers to tell me who my family is," I say.

"We won't be your run-of-the-mill family. I mean, we're not even under the same roof."

"Think about it, Ed; would you and Miranda really want to live with Aunt Millie and Drew?"

Ed laughs. "You have a point." I pause, feeling a bit awkward. These heart-to-heart talks with Ed will take some getting used to.

"You're not disappointed?" I ask just as the conductor calls out, "All aboard!"

"Disappointed?"

"You know, because I'm going to stay at Aunt Millie's, too." I kick the platform with my shoe. "It's just…well…I don't really need anyone to adopt me." I used to think it would be easy, never seeing Aunt Millie again, especially those times when we squabble over things, but it's complicated. And then there's Evelyn to consider. Bad enough I'm away at school, how would I tell him I was moving to Sheppard Square? We'd probably never see each other again. At the rate he's going, the doctor says he'll be back to his old self in no time. Even so, that doesn't mean I'm going to turn my back on him. Miss Turner was right about true friends being like diamonds.

"Just so long as you know you can change your mind at any time," says Ed, smiling down at me. "There will always be a room for you at our house.... Now, you'd better get on that train before it takes off without you." I pick up my bag and start walking away. The January wind whips up across the platform, pulling at my coat. Turning back, I can make out Ed still standing where I left him. I set my bag down and hurry back, throw my arms around his waist, and bury my face into the warmth of his overcoat. His hand rests on the back of my head. It feels so good.

—

Life is a book of volumes three;
The past, the present, the future to be.
The past is written and laid away;
The present is writing day by day;
The future — oh, what can it be?
God only knows he holds the key.

I've been thinking a lot about the verse I wrote in Jennie's autograph book — mostly that line about the past being written and laid away. All my life I couldn't put my past away because I didn't know any of the things that had been written there. I guess maybe you need to know what that past is before you can put it away once and for all. I used to think that finding my mother would make me happy, but now I know that's not true. Now that I finally know what my past is, I'm not sure what difference it makes to the person I am today. One thing I've learned about the past: whether it's the one you know or the one you don't, there's still a way to put it to rest. I didn't find out who my mother is, but at least I know my story. It might not be the one I dreamed up in my head, but it's mine all the same. Some things you have to be okay with because you have no choice in the matter. All the lies Aunt Millie concocted, all the stories she told over the years, none of it changes who I am. Still, it would have been better to know the truth right from the start.

"What colour's the page?" asked Jennie.

"My favourite colour — blue," I said. I read her the verse and she seemed pleased to pieces. She had it memorized in no time flat. I got if from Mrs. Merry over the Christmas vacation. She heard me telling Evelyn that I needed a verse. She brought out her old autograph book and let me look through it. It seemed kind of fitting, seeing how Evelyn and I have both laid away some things from the past. As soon as I read it, I knew it was the one.

—

Morning assembly is about to start. The line starts moving. I grab fast to Nessa's hand as we move along.

"So what happened over Christmas? Did you find out the truth about your mother? I'm dying to know," she says, slipping a jawbreaker into my hand.

I look at her and smile.

"The mystery of Cammie Turple is finally solved," I say, popping the candy into my mouth.

The little bird in my chest is happily fluttering its wings.

Author's Note

In Cammie's day, blind and visually impaired children in the Atlantic provinces had the opportunity to attend the Halifax School for the Blind. It was the first residential school for the blind in Canada; a home away from home for the children who lived there ten months out of the year. Blind students were taught to read and write Braille while sighted students, like Cammie, read from large-print books. The school taught a regular curriculum and offered a variety of skills designed to help place these students in the workforce later in life. Some of these included: knitting, basketry, croqueting and sewing for the girls; piano tuning, chair caning, and woodworking for the boys. At the time of this story, Mr. Allen was the name of the Superintendent, but the names of all the other staff are a product of my imagination. The school stood on the corner of University Avenue and South Park Street and closed in 1983.

The Ideal Maternity Home in East Chester, Nova Scotia would have been in operation at the time of Cammie's birth. It was run by William and Lila Young. Many of the babies, born to unwed mothers at the home, were adopted out. However, it is alleged that the babies considered unadoptable, because of health issues or even the colour of their skin, were neglected and starved to death. The home burned to the ground in 1962.

Today, monuments mark the spot where the Ideal Maternity Home in East Chester and the Halifax School for the Blind once stood.

Acknowledgements

I am so grateful for the continued support and encouragement from my family, friends, and community. It means a great deal to have so many people in my corner.

A special thanks to Nimbus Publishing, especially Whitney Moran and Penelope Jackson for their editorial guidance. It's been a joy to work with both of you on this book.

To Penny Ferguson and the editors of the *Amethyst Review* for publishing my very first short story over twenty years ago: thanks for giving a new writer a start.

My thanks to Jan Coates for reading a few early chapters and offering your bits of wisdom; our Vittles coffee dates continue to inspire me to keep writing.

My thanks to Syr Ruus for your wise and always witty observations. You are an inspiration to other writers.

Special thanks to Brian for being my chauffeur, my sounding board, my greatest supporter.

Thanks to my mum and stepdad for sharing your experiences at the Halifax School for the Blind, and for helping me understand not only the limitations of your world but your many abilities as well. Mum, I grew up hearing stories about Edith, Goldie, Barb, and Latisha and it was those stories that inspired me to write this book. I only wish they could all be here to share in Cammie's story. Harold, thanks for sharing your own unique experience at the school. The boys certainly seemed to have been an adventuresome lot!

Finally, to all those who attended the Halifax School for the Blind, I hope I managed to create a realistic portrayal of a visually impaired girl learning to navigate her way in a sighted world.

SHELLEY ZINCK

LAURA BEST has had over forty short stories published in literary magazines and anthologies. Her first young adult novel, *Bitter, Sweet,* was shortlisted for the Geoffrey Bilson Award for Historical Fiction for Young People and made the Best Books for Kids and Teens 2011 list. Her most recent book, *Flying with a Broken Wing,* was named one of Bank Street College of Education's Best Books of 2015. She lives in East Dalhousie, Nova Scotia, with her husband, Brian. Visit lauraabest.wordpress.com.